Fabulous Fathers

"That was the tackiest wedding I've ever attended," the new bride said.

Jonas laughed. "Fly to Vegas, deposit a fee and withdraw a marriage certificate. Pretty convenient."

Robin sighed. "But a drive-through wedding chapel?" she asked. "I felt like I was going to the bank."

"Hey," Jonas replied, "our nuptials may have been as tacky as a polyester leisure suit, but it solved my problem."

His choice of words hit her wrong, and Robin swung her gaze to her new husband.

"Our problem," he quickly amended.

Dear Reader,

What happens when six brides and six grooms wed for *convenient* reasons? Well... In Donna Clayton's *Daddy Down the Aisle*, a confirmed bachelor becomes a FABULOUS FATHER—with the love of an adorable toddler...and his beautiful bride.

One night of passion leaves a (usually) prim woman expecting a BUNDLE OF JOY! In Sandra Steffen's *For Better, For Baby*, the mom-to-be marries the dad-to-be—and now they have nine months to fall in love....

From secretarial pool to wife of the handsome boss! Well, for a while. In Alaina Hawthorne's *Make-Believe Bride*, she hopes to be his Mrs. Forever—after all, that's how long she's loved him!

What's a rancher to do when his ex-wife turns up on his doorstep with amnesia and a big, juicy kiss? In Val Whisenand's *Temporary Husband*, he simply "forgets" to remind her that they're divorced....

Disguised as lovey-dovey newlyweds on a honeymoon at the Triple Fork Ranch, not-so-loving police partners uncover their own wedded bliss in Laura Anthony's *Undercover Honeymoon*....

In debut author Cathy Forsythe's *The Marriage Contract*, a sexy cowboy proposes a marriage of convenience, but when his bride discovers the real reason he said "I do"— watch out!

I hope you enjoy all six of our wonderful CONVENIENTLY WED titles this month—and all of the Silhouette Romance novels to come!

Regards,

Melissa Senate
Senior Editor

Please address questions and book requests to:
Silhouette Reader Service
U.S.: 3010 Walden Ave., P.O. Box 1325, Buffalo, NY 14269
Canadian: P.O. Box 609, Fort Erie, Ont. L2A 5X3

DADDY DOWN THE AISLE

Donna Clayton

Conveniently
Wed

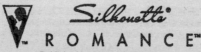

Silhouette®
R O M A N C E™
Published by Silhouette Books
America's Publisher of Contemporary Romance

For those wonderful ladies of the
Delaware Chapter of RWA.
Thanks for the endless love and support.

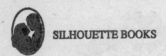 SILHOUETTE BOOKS

ISBN 0-373-19162-6

DADDY DOWN THE AISLE

Copyright © 1996 by Donna Fasano

This edition published by arrangement with Harlequin Books S.A.

Printed in U.S.A.

DONNA CLAYTON

is proud to be a recipient of the HOLT Medallion, an award honoring Outstanding Literary Talent. And seeing her work appear on the Waldenbooks Series Bestsellers List has given her a great deal of joy and satisfaction.

Reading is one of Donna's favorite ways to while away a rainy afternoon. She loves to hike, too. Another hobby added to her list of fun things to do is traveling. She fell in love with Europe during her first trip abroad recently and plans to return often. Oh, and Donna still collects cookbooks, but as her writing career grows, she finds herself using them less and less.

VOWS FROM THE NEW FATHER

I, Jonas Winslow, take you, Anthony, to be my son. I really want to do well in my new daddy role, but you've got to understand that all this fatherhood stuff is new to me. So that's why I've asked your aunt Robin to be my wife. Can you believe I've actually gotten married? I hope that together——if we don't drive each other nutty first——we'll be able to give you all the love you deserve.

VOWS FROM THE NEW MOTHER

I, Robin Hampstead Winslow, take you, Anthony, as my child. Although I haven't seen you in several months, you've never been out of my thoughts. I know your uncle has been taking great care of you, but I'll feel better being around all the time——which is why I've agreed to marry Jonas. I hope that eventually you'll be able to call me Mama, just as I hope Jonas will someday call me wife . . . and mean it.

Prologue

"My brother did *what?*" Robin Hampstead clutched the telephone receiver in her fist until her knuckles turned into little white knobs. Her insides trembled as she stared out the sliding glass door of her hotel room, but the tropical beauty of Hawaii lent her none of the serenity it had since her arrival.

"Robin—" the elderly female voice on the other end of the phone line held a calming intonation "—I want you to stop and take a deep breath. It hasn't even been twenty-four hours since you found out about Jeff and Sara's...accident."

Swallowing around the painful lump of emotion in her throat, Robin closed her eyes and took a shaky inhalation. Her brother and his wife were dead. The realization had hardly had a chance to sink in. Robin's teeth clenched tight against the agonizing ache in her chest.

The person on the other end of the telephone was a friend, she reminded herself. It was okay to express to

Lynn all the overwhelming grief she was feeling over the sudden death of Jeff and Sara. But, once again, Robin found herself unable to confide her innermost feelings.

"Sit down," Lynn softly commanded.

Robin's knees bent of their own volition and she sank onto the upholstered chair beside the desk. Her mind raced with a thousand questions—questions that weren't able to form completely before being overrun by another and another. It was impossible to think coherently.

"I knew I shouldn't have opened your letter."

Lynn seemed to be talking to herself, and although the woman's voice barely penetrated her wretched stupor, Robin felt the instinctive urge to comfort her.

"But I asked you to." The words sounded rusty and grating to Robin's ears. "There wasn't time to forward it. And there won't be time for me to stop in New York." It seemed as though someone else was speaking instead of herself, so distant and hushed was her voice. "I'll be flying straight to Baltimore and then renting a car..."

"Has the storm cleared enough for the airport to open?" Lynn asked.

"Not yet. All the airlines are still on standby."

Lynn sighed. "It won't be long. You'll be on your way soon."

She swallowed with difficulty. "I'm all packed. I have all my notes together about the restaurants I visited. And what recipes I could gather. Some chefs are so protective. I'm sure I have enough information to finish the article."

Dear Lord, she was babbling. Her nerves were frayed and her thinking hazy to the point that she was talking nonsense. Who cared if she wrote the article or not? The editors at *Fancy Food* would understand, wouldn't they? She'd just been notified of a death in her immediate family....

Immediate family. To most people, those two words meant warm, close ties. But to Robin... Suddenly the cold, empty loneliness that engulfed her was not only overwhelming, but it was also frightening.

"Oh, Lynn—" suppressed emotion crackled in her voice like erratic sparks "—I hope I arrive in time for the memorial service."

She heard her friend heave a commiserating sigh.

"It seems all the arrangements were stipulated in your brother's will," Lynn said. "No funeral. And a memorial service for family and friends to be held within forty-eight hours of..." Here she let the sentence fade with yet another sigh.

The original purpose of Lynn's call came to mind, clearing up some of the fog that had enveloped Robin's brain. She tipped up her chin. Her voice seemed to gain strength as she said, "Read the letter again, Lynn. The important part, anyway."

Lynn cleared her throat with a gravelly sound. "You have been named by Jeffrey Aaron Hampstead and Sara Marie Hampstead as coguardian of Anthony Aaron Hampstead—"

"Little Tony," Robin whispered.

She fought back the panic that welled in her chest, but like unrelenting waves crashing against the sandy beach, her anxiety built higher and higher.

"I don't know anything about babies, Lynn," she said. "I've only been out of college three years. Traveling all over the place." Her insides began to quake. "I don't have a home. I rent a room, for goodness' sake. Where am I going to keep a baby?"

An unbidden memory swamped her, and suddenly she was back at little Tony's christening feeling awkward and clumsy and extremely inadequate as she held her brother's child in her arms. She remembered how hurt she felt as Jeff, Sara and Jonas Winslow, Sara's brother, had laughed at her lack of maternal instincts. She'd been embarrassed by their good-natured jeering, but Robin had to admit that their opinions had been correct—she didn't have an ounce of knowledge where children were concerned.

"That poor little boy would be at a terrible disadvantage having me as his—" She stopped abruptly. "How am I ever going to—" Again she stopped. "I couldn't possibly continue to travel—" Her breath seemed to catch in her throat and she gasped, failing to keep her hysteria at bay. "What's going to happen when—"

"Robin, stop this," Lynn softly chided. "Everything's going to be okay. The letter said *co*guardian." She emphasized the prefix.

"Yes, yes," Robin whispered, latching on to this small ray of hope with both hands.

"Do you have any idea who else might be named?"

Robin nodded vigorously even though Lynn was thousands of miles away and unable to see through the telephone lines. "Sara's parents," she said emphatically. "My brother's in-laws live in the same small town. I'm sure it's them."

"The baby's grandparents," Lynn said. "See there, you have nothing to worry about. Grandparents love their grandchildren."

Again, Robin found herself nodding. "Mr. and Mrs. Winslow do love Tony." Relief flooded her until she thought she'd cry, but she succeeded in warding off the tears. "And they're very nice people. I met them at Jeff and Sara's wedding and then again at Tony's christening."

"You have nothing to worry about then, do you? The little fella's grandparents have experience with children, and he knows them. He's comfortable with them." Her words lightened considerably. "There should be no reason you can't continue traveling for the magazine."

Robin thought a moment. "It would probably make things easier for Mr. and Mrs. Winslow if I were to sign over all rights to them. I mean, I trust them implicitly to take good care of the baby."

"When you stay calm," Lynn commented gently, "all kinds of options come to mind."

Now it was Robin's turn to sigh. "I feel so much better about this whole thing."

Jonas Winslow reread the letter he'd received from his sister's lawyer, and then let it fall atop the scatter of penciled drawings on his desk. His heart ached for Sara. He had so many wonderful memories of growing up as her big brother. They'd been close, he and Sara. And he'd always been extremely protective of her. Yet, when Jeff Hampstead had come along, he'd stepped aside and let the love of his sister's life take over. He'd liked Jeff. Had even come to think of him as the brother he'd never had. And now they both were gone.

Sadness prickled behind his eyelids, threatening to take the shape of tears. He sniffed and rubbed firm fingers across his jaw. He hadn't time to grieve. There were too many arrangements for the memorial service to attend to, too many phone calls that had to be made.

The sound of his mother's sobs came back to haunt him. With the condition his father was in, Jonas knew there was no way his mother could leave him to fly up for Sara's memorial service. She'd tearfully suggested a home nurse, and then immediately rejected the idea, knowing how her husband became so easily disoriented and frightened these days. Besides, neither of them had been in the retirement village long enough to even get settled yet. Jonas had tried to console his mother and had finally convinced her that staying in Florida with his dad was the best thing.

When his mother had asked after the baby, Jonas had explained how Sara's best friend, Amy, had called and offered to keep Tony until he could make arrangements for the memorial service. He needed to call his mother again sometime today.

He gazed down at the document that sat on top of the disorganized pile of articles in various stages of editing and he thought of his fourteen-month-old nephew. The memory of the child's wide-eyed, frightened gaze had preyed on Jonas's mind—no matter how hard he tried, he couldn't exorcise the image of those huge, teary brown eyes as Tony had called out longingly for his mother.

The lump of emotion that rose in Jonas's throat nearly choked him. He coughed, pushed himself to his feet and paced the room.

He wanted to do the right thing by Sara and Jeff. Hell, that's why he'd worked so hard to quickly pull together a decent memorial service. Jonas had no idea why the two of them had stipulated that the service be held within such a short time period, but he'd done all he could to abide by their wishes.

Yes, he wanted to do the right thing by Sara and Jeff. And little Tony. But Jonas had to admit, if to no one but himself, that there couldn't be a worse time for him to take on the responsibilities of a child.

He gazed over at the file cabinet and thought of the brand-new, multibook contract he'd signed—a contract that called for all new, never-before-published material. The next year was going to be very busy if he was going to create new material for a book *and* keep up with his daily syndication demands. How was he ever going to work and take care of Tony at the same time?

As he searched through his brain for possible solutions, he dragged his fingers through his hair and realized just how badly he needed it cut. He looked around his office at the messy piles of computer paper, research books, newspapers, and empty coffee mugs. A blunt-tipped pencil sat forgotten on the floor in the corner of the room. A thick layer of dust covered the file cabinet. He wondered how long it had been since he'd cleaned the place. And then his stomach rumbled softly, alerting him that he hadn't eaten since late yesterday.

"How can I possibly take care of a baby when I can't even remember to take care of myself?" The words were harsh and grated with self-disgust. He went to his desk and picked up a small, framed photograph of his nephew.

"Tony," he whispered to the picture, "you deserve better than what your uncle Jonas has to offer."

As he stared down at the boy's image, he wondered how life could be so cruel to one so young. Tony's little bow-shaped mouth curled into a tiny smile so like his mother's. The child had gotten his carrot-red hair and big brown eyes from his father. Sadness and grief welled inside Jonas, making his chest tight, his breathing ragged. His vision became blurred with the moisture that gathered in his eyes. He blinked several times, hard, then pressed his thumb and index finger against his closed lids.

He put the picture down and inhaled deeply. There had to be an answer to this time dilemma of his regarding his work and taking custody of his nephew.

Jonas had to confess that he'd been surprised when he'd received the letter informing him that he'd been named as Tony's guardian. He guessed Sara just wanted him to know that she loved him and was thinking of him. As a bachelor, Jonas spent very little time around children. In fact, his nephew had been the one and only child he'd ever been around. But he loved the boy. Loved to drop by unexpectedly to see what havoc the little fellow was wreaking on his sister and brother-in-law's household. So, realizing his lack of experience with children, he *had* been taken off guard to learn that Sara wanted him to help raise her son.

But it was the *co*guardianship that intrigued him. And he also realized that it was the *co*guardianship that would be his saving grace. He wasn't going to be in this alone. And the fact that there was someone else who would be responsible for the baby along with himself might be the answer to his problem.

Although he hadn't had a chance to talk to her, Jonas knew that the other person named by his sister would be Amy, the lady who was watching his nephew right now. Sara's best friend would be the perfect person to raise Tony. The woman was part of a strong and happy marriage, which was really an amazing feat in these days and times. And Amy was a wonderful mother with two adorable children of her own. He'd seen Amy and her husband in parental action at Tony's first birthday party two months ago and they'd been wonderful with their kids.

Hell, for all Jonas knew, Amy and her husband could both be named as coguardians along with him. *Co* didn't have to stop at two. It simply meant more than one.

He could explain his problem about his new book contract to Amy and her husband. They'd understand. And they would work with him, he was certain.

But then again, he could be entirely wrong. He leaned his elbow on top of the dusty file cabinet, a deep frown planting itself in his brow. It could be that Sara and Jeff didn't have Amy in mind as the guardian of their son. Jeff *did* have a sister....

Before the idea could even take shape in his mind, Jonas dismissed it. He thought back to Tony's christening day. Robin Hampstead had looked so ill at ease as she'd held the baby. Even now, Jonas found himself chuckling aloud at the memory despite his melancholy mood.

He easily recalled Robin's image: her flame-red hair had been short and curly, her cute little nose upturned, and those large brown eyes so quick to flash in anger. She was young, in her mid-twenties, he guessed. But her serious nature made her seem years older. She was a career woman through and through. The very kind he loved to poke fun at in his work. A smile tugged at his mouth as he thought of how easy it had been to rile her. She hadn't liked him. She'd made that plain enough. And she'd told him his opinion pieces were a waste of good paper. Yes, he thought, chuckling again, he'd had some good fun the day he'd spent with Robin Hampstead.

But his sister, Sara, had told him that Robin didn't have a maternal bone in her body. Sara would never consider her sister-in-law good mother material for Tony. And Robin's total lack of any sense of humor actually made him shudder.

No, Jonas was certain that Sara would choose Amy over Robin any day of the week. Amy was the sensible choice. Hell, she was the *only* choice as far as he could see. He was sure that Sara and Jeff would feel the same. Besides that, Amy was certain to be understanding where his work schedule was concerned. Things would work out just fine.

He heaved a great sigh. He was beginning to feel better about this whole situation.

Chapter One

Robin rushed up the steps of the small church, finger-combing her wayward curls as she went. Stopping at the entrance, she took a moment to steel herself and shake the droplets of spring rain from the shoulders of her coat before she eased open the heavy door and slipped inside. The tiny, windowless vestibule was cool and dark, and she found herself squinting and blinking until her eyes became adjusted to the light change. Her gaze was drawn to a small lamp that sat on a flat-topped podium, its low-wattage bulb throwing a ray of dim light on an elegant white register. She neatly signed her name and replaced the pen into its holder.

The sound of perfectly harmonized voices suddenly filled the air. Robin followed the beautiful singing into the interior of the church. She halted just inside the doorway, a huge lump rising in her throat at the sight of the crowded room. These people were friends to Jeff and Sara. All these people loved and cared about her brother and his wife. All of them had come to remember.

Feeling trembly all of a sudden, Robin slid into an empty spot in the very back of the church. She scrambled around in her purse for a tissue, and when she couldn't find one, the woman next to her offered one along with a small smile. Robin nodded her thanks.

She relaxed against the back of the pew, closed her eyes and let the music of the choir flow all around her and through her chaotic mind. She'd made it. She'd actually arrived in Brenville in time for the memorial service. And it was a small miracle that she had. Of course, now there was a seventy-two-dollar speeding ticket that had to be paid. But, despite that, she said a quick prayer of thanks that she hadn't missed the service.

Jonas watched Robin from his seat at the front of the church. The minister had offered for him to sit in the very front pew—the usual place for family members—but Jonas had known that he would have been there all alone and opted to position himself opposite the choir. He'd used the excuse that he needed to be within easy reach of the dais when it was his turn to speak. From this vantage point in front of the church, he could see the comings and goings of the attendees.

He'd seen Jeff's sister arrive—thirty minutes into the service. Her fiery red hair had caught his attention as soon as she'd stepped over the threshold of the sanctuary. She hadn't come up front to the family pew, but had taken a seat at the back.

The minister of the church stood to speak, but Jonas only half heard the words. Robin looked tired, he observed. The dark circles under her deep-set eyes gave her a haunting look. He'd only met the woman twice—he'd never forget either encounter—but seeing her again brought to his mind the same observation that there was something lonely, something isolated about her solemn nature. He remembered how both times he'd met her, there had been something about her that had kept her in his thoughts for days and weeks after the experience. He'd found himself puzzling over what it was that so intrigued him about her, until finally he'd become angry with himself for wasting time on the woman and put her out of his mind. Hell, he ultimately concluded, why throw away perfectly good brainpower on someone who didn't even *like* him?

Her eyelids slowly rose and the haunting look turned into a mixture of something tragic and ethereal all at the same time. He found the combination lovely, almost . . seductive.

You're sick, Winslow, he told himself. *The woman's grieving, for goodness' sake.* But he continued to study her as she gazed up at the large stained-glass image above the altar.

He'd been told that she was on assignment in Hawaii and assured that she'd been contacted about the accident, but Jonas couldn't help worrying during the past forty-eight hours about whether or not she'd be able to fly across an ocean and then the country to arrive in time. Well, he was glad to see that attending her brother's memorial service meant a little more to her than her precious career.

Now, that's not fair, a silent inner voice scolded. And he knew it was true. Robin Hampstead might be a career woman, but that didn't mean she wasn't a decent human being. She must have loved her brother just as much as he had loved his sister, Sara. His nerves were frayed, his emotions in turmoil over this loss, and that was the only excuse he had to explain his mean and petty assessment of Robin's late arrival.

When Jonas noticed that Reverend Walsh had gone silent, he turned his gaze to the man to see the minister motion him forward. Jonas felt his face flame with embarrassment. If he'd been paying attention instead of focusing his thoughts on Robin Hampstead, he'd have been prepared to speak rather than being taken off guard. He rose, tugged on the hem of his jacket and made his way to the dais.

Seeing Jonas Winslow cross the altar area, Robin almost groaned aloud. If he made some kind of wisecrack about Jeff and Sara, she'd just scream. Both times Robin had met Sara's brother, the man had infuriated her with his jeering and critical remarks. Nothing was safe from his black humor.

Robin remembered that Jonas had made asinine comments about Sara and Jeff's relationship at the wedding. Her own career had been fodder for his jokes that same day. He'd even used Tony's christening, an event that should have been serious and sacred, and he'd turned the day into material for his dark satire. That was also the day that Jonas had embarrassed her beyond rational thought—

"Today is a day of celebration..."

His voice broke into her dark musings, and she was so startled by his choice of words that her chin tipped upward and her eyes became glued to his face. She made a conscious effort to keep her mouth from dropping open. If this was his idea of a joke... She didn't finish the thought when she realized that she wasn't the only one surprised by his statement, for the room grew utterly quiet and still as everyone waited for him to continue.

"Sara and Jeff didn't want us to mourn their passing," he said. "They didn't want us, their family and friends, to gather together for a sad and somber affair. They didn't want a funeral.''

Robin watched Jonas inhale deeply, and she could tell that it took a great deal of control and effort for him to pull the corners of his mouth into a tiny smile.

"Sara and Jeff,'' he continued, ''didn't want us to feel miserable or brokenhearted by their passing. Of course . . . we will.'' His tone quivered slightly as he added the aside. "But my sister and her husband wanted us—'' He faltered, cleared his throat, and when he began again, his words were stronger, more vibrant. "It was their wish that we celebrate today by recounting our memories of them.''

Robin closed her eyes. His words were beautiful, she had to admit. And the whole idea of celebrating her brother and sister-in-law through memories was beautiful, too.

"Sara and Jeff loved each and every one of us,'' Jonas said. "They knew we would all have a need to grieve for them. But it was important to them that we do it as joyously and . . . cheerfully as possible.''

Sitting there in the back of the church, Robin let herself become wrapped in the warm, comforting cocoon of Jonas's tone. She'd forgotten how deep, how rich . . . how memorable his voice was. The acoustics in the high-ceilinged church amplified the melodic pitch of his slightly Southern accent. His words were inflected with an intense resonance that seemed to smooth across her mind, across her skin as if it were warm, liquid velvet.

"We've enjoyed some beautiful music sung by the choir,'' he said. "These songs were some of Jeff and Sara's very favorites.'' This time his smile was fond and didn't have to be forced. "I know that from now until the end of my life I will remember them both whenever I hear these melodies.'' He looked toward the front pews. "Several of

Sara's friends have asked to speak. They have biblical readings and poetry they would like to share. And some of Jeff's friends and co-workers would like to relate some of their thoughts."

As soon as the first person stepped up to the dais to speak, the weird feeling began. Robin listened to the lyrical psalms, the beautiful poetry, but the thoughts and feelings these people expressed started to form a strange emptiness inside her. She was surprised by the number of people who rose to speak, and soon Robin realized that this wasn't part of the planned service. These men and women didn't want to wait until after the memorial service to express the love they felt for Jeff and Sara. These people wanted to be included in this most intimate memorial tribute.

One by one, friends of Sara and Jeff verbalized their fondest memories of the deceased couple. Some of these memories were sad, some funny, some ironic, but all were poignant. And with each remembrance, Robin found herself learning something new about her brother and his wife. With each remembrance, Robin discovered how little she knew about Jeff and Sara.

Her chin quivered as the huge, black void inside her yawned wide. The small church didn't seem big enough to hold her and the emptiness she felt. Suddenly the room seemed as though it were closing in on her. She felt the need to flee. But at the same time, she wanted to stay. As the affectionate, soul-stirring reminiscences flowed, Robin wanted so badly to pluck them from the air and clutch them to her, have them as her very own. But that was impossible.

She pressed her fingers against her lips, trying to hold back the lonely sobs that threatened to choke her. No, she couldn't have these memories. They belonged to other people—people who *knew* Jeff and Sara. Her mind whirled with sadness and confusion as yet another story about her brother was recounted, and the ever-widening hollowness swelled until she thought she'd fall into its black, bottomless depths.

Instinct screamed at her; if she couldn't snatch up some of these wonderful memories to fill this emptiness expanding inside her, then she needed to somehow avoid them. Hide from them. Run from them.

Her gaze darted around the room, and as she saw that there was actually a small line of people now forming at the front of the church, she fought the urge to press her hands over her ears. Again, instinct screamed for her to flee. Gathering her purse, Robin surrendered to impulse, and escaped.

Later that afternoon, Robin entered the building that housed the offices of the family court. Before she'd left Hawaii, she'd been informed by her friend Lynn that there was to be a meeting with a court clerk.

Robin had spent two hours sitting in a small coffee-house frantically trying to ignore the vacant feeling inside her. She'd focused her thoughts on Tony, and she'd re-affirmed her conclusion that she was probably the worst person to raise the child.

Yes, she could ask the magazine to give her a job where travel wasn't expected. But her job was the least of her reasons for feeling inadequate to be the baby's guardian. She knew nothing about children. Nothing. And even worse than that, Robin had come to understand the stark reality that she knew nothing about her nephew's parents. She wouldn't be able to tell the child anything about his mom and dad. Handing over full rights to Sara's parents was the best thing for her to do for her brother's son.

Pulling open the glass door, she went inside. Her heels clicked a steady, hollow rhythm on the tiled hallway floor. She spied a sign for the ladies' room and followed the arrow.

The air had that sweet, bubble-gum smell of just-scrubbed public rest rooms. She looked in the mirror over the sink and nearly groaned aloud. The light spring rain had drenched her to the skin. Her usually bright red hair was darkened to auburn by the dampness. Pulling a comb from her purse, she ran it through her curls, but they seemed to spring back with a life of their own and she gave up.

She looked gaunt and hollow-eyed, and she reached up to try to pinch some color into her cheeks. She regretted not staying for the gathering after the memorial service to see Sara's parents and Tony. She hadn't seen them at the church at all, but she'd figured that they were sitting up front. But she'd see all three of them in just a few minutes. She hoped her pale-as-a-ghost complexion didn't frighten the baby.

The office was easy to find. She'd taken the stairs to the second floor, found the correct door and knocked.

"Come in," a muffled voice called.

Robin opened the door and smiled at the young woman—the *very* young woman—who sat behind the gray metal desk.

"Hi," she said, her voice as perky as her smile. She stood and offered her hand. "I'm Alice McCarthy."

Robin introduced herself and said, "I hope I'm in the right place."

"Oh, yes," Alice told her. "I was just looking over the file. You're a little early. Have a seat."

Robin perched herself on the very edge of the seat. "I'm glad I'm early," she said. "I'm glad I have the chance to explain what I've planned to do about my nephew." She paused only an instant before continuing. "You see, I've decided to sign over all rights to Sara's parents. I think they'll make excellent guardians for Tony."

The bewildered frown on Alice's face didn't even register with Robin, so intent was she on justifying her actions.

"You see," she repeated, clenching her hands in her lap, "I know so little about children. My job takes me all over the world." She tried to swallow and realized how cottony her mouth felt. "I want you to understand that it's not that I don't love Tony, it's just that..." She felt wretched inside. "I've never had anyone depend on me before."

The truth was she'd never *wanted* anyone to depend on her. The very idea frightened her to the core.

Robin searched the face of the young court clerk and prayed that the woman would understand. Silent seconds ticked by and Robin wished Alice would say something, anything.

"Well," the young woman began slowly, "I'm a little confused about what you want to do."

Before Robin could respond, the door to the small office opened.

Alice stood and smiled at the man who entered the room. "You must be Mr. Winslow," she said. "I'm Alice McCarthy."

So surprised by Jonas's appearance, Robin suddenly became paralyzed as questions swam through her brain. What was *he* doing here? Had he been named coguardian, too? But where were Sara's parents? How could Jeff and Sara have chosen *him* to—

"Yes. I'm here about the guardianship of my nephew, Tony Hampstead."

Robin forced herself to raise her gaze to his face. The door hid most of him, but she saw a tiny slice of his profile. It seemed that he wasn't yet aware of her presence, and Robin was relieved by that fact. She could use another moment or two to pull herself together.

"Well, come in, Mr. Winslow," Alice said.

"Jonas," he said. "Call me Jonas."

Unwittingly Robin's hand went up to smooth over her damp, unruly curls. If Jonas Winslow—a man who trivialized every aspect of life—was named as the other co-guardian, that changed everything. She couldn't possibly let this snide, disrespectful man raise her nephew. She couldn't possibly—

"Have a seat, Jonas," Alice said. "As you can see, Ms. Hampstead has already arrived. Since we're all here, we might as well discuss the situation."

"Oh..."

There was surprise in his green gaze. Surprise and something else, something she couldn't interpret. But she had no doubt that her presence had taken him off guard. *Well, good,* she thought. Because his unexpected appearance had done the same to her.

"But..." His voice trailed and a frown planted itself firmly between his brows. He turned his full attention to stepping into the room and closing the door, an act that seemed to take more time than it should have.

When he looked at her again, there was something in his eyes, something she couldn't quite name. But whatever it was caused the air in the room to become so filled with tension that it was hard for her to draw a breath. She could feel herself becoming flustered. Damn, why did she let this man do this to her every time they met?

She would not allow him to make her feel embarrassed and awkward. Not this time.

Tipping up her chin, she said, "I've never seen you at a loss for words, Jonas."

Her statement had been tinged with sarcasm, and it acted like a good douse of water on a small camp fire, diffusing the strain that had sprung up so suddenly. His lips curled slightly into a crooked smile—a *sexy,* crooked smile, she thought not for the first time in her life. And not for the first time in her life, she felt her stomach tilt at the sight of it. She swallowed hard. She refused to let herself become rattled by his good looks.

"Hello, Robin," he said.

"Jonas."

"So," Alice chimed in, her tone evincing her relief, "you two *do* know each other. I was beginning to wonder."

"Oh, we know each other," Jonas assured her.

"Well, that's good." The court clerk motioned to the chair. "Sit, sit," she told him. "Let's talk. We have lots to go over, and Ms. Hampstead was just telling me how she was thinking of signing over all rights to—"

"B-but wait," Robin stammered in a rush. "That was before..." Her heart pounded in her chest. "That was when I thought..." How could she say this without offending him? She tried again. "That was—"

"Before you knew I was the other coguardian?" One of Jonas's dark brows rose with his question.

Somehow, having him finish her thought made it sound even worse than her saying the words herself. But he'd captured her idea exactly.

His mouth curled into that smile again and she felt her insides grow all warm and...funny.

"I'll be honest," he said. "I'm more than a little surprised to see *you* here."

"Oh? And why is that?" she said, a waspish tone in her voice. "*If* you don't mind my asking."

Immediately she realized her mistake, and she felt the urge to kick herself for rising to his bait.

The court clerk crinkled the papers she held in her hand, and when that didn't get her the attention she wanted, she cleared her throat. "Now, let's just calm down," she said, sounding as authoritarian as was possible.

"Yes, Robin," Jonas agreed wholeheartedly. "Can't you see the girl wants to speak?"

"The *woman* wants to speak," Robin snapped as she crossed her arms in front of her chest. She was fuming, and what riled her even more was the fact that she couldn't figure out with whom she was more angry—Jonas or herself! Why did this man's smug tone infuriate her so? she wondered. Why did she let him get under her skin? And why did he have to do it when she was sitting here looking like a drowned rat?

She stopped and blinked. Why did it matter *what* she looked like? Why did she care? The questions burned through her brain. Why was she so angry, anyway? All the man had done was voice her own thoughts for her. She didn't know why she was so incensed. Couldn't come up with a logical reason. Well, logic be damned! All she knew was that she was steaming like a whistling teakettle.

"Surprised to see me," she muttered under her breath, unable to let go of the irritation he'd induced. "And who was it you were expecting?" she mumbled. "I *am* Jeff's only sister, you know. I'm all the family he had."

He turned his green-eyed gaze on her. "Let me get this straight. You're Jeff's only relative, yet you're ready to give up guardianship of his son." He snorted in a most ungentlemanly manner. "What? Would a baby cramp the career woman's style?"

"My job has nothing to do with this."

"Please stop!" Alice's tone of voice and her facial features took on a plaintive, beseeching quality. "Don't argue. This is my first case ever, and I wanted to do a good job."

Jonas heard the whiny court clerk, but he didn't take his eyes from Robin's face. There were rings under her deepset, chocolate brown eyes. She looked tired. And angry. Why was he harassing her? he wondered. He had certainly meant to be compassionate when he came face-to-face with her. He sighed. The woman just had a way of rubbing him the wrong way.

He'd been taken completely off guard when he realized she was the other coguardian. He'd been expecting Sara's best friend, Amy. He'd even talked to Amy this morning, told her that he'd meet her here at family court. She was to bring Tony with her. She hadn't refuted anything he'd said, she'd simply agreed to everything. Of course they had both been in a rush, but naturally, he'd believed that she was the other guardian. Then to find Robin Hampstead sitting here . . . No wonder he'd been taken by surprise.

And now Robin was staring him down, her mouth set in a grim line. This situation couldn't have gotten off to a worse start.

Turning to the befuddled young woman behind the desk, Jonas conjured a charming smile. "Alice," he said. "It is Alice, isn't it?"

"Yes."

She nodded like an eager puppy, obviously desperate for a solution to the messy problem that had somehow developed.

"Well, Alice, it seems that Robin and I were both a little surprised by the other's presence."

"Oh, but I thought I mentioned both your names in the letter I sent to you." Apologetic innocence colored her statement and she searched through the papers on her desk. "Oh," she said, looking crestfallen when she'd found her copies of said letters, "I'm so sorry."

"It's okay," Jonas assured her. "Since this is your first case—" he chuckled "—we'll cut you a little slack. Won't we, Robin?"

Robin's smile was forced as she continued to glare at him. "Of course we will."

"See there," he said. "Now, if you'll give Robin and I some time to talk..."

"That's an excellent idea." The clerk hopped up and almost slipped in her haste to get to the door. She pulled it open and it banged into the metal chair Jonas was sitting in, but when she turned back to them, she didn't waste time with apologies. "Please don't fight," she begged. "If you get too loud I'll have to call for security, and that wouldn't look too good for me...seeing as how this is—"

"Your first case," Jonas finished for her. "We'll be on our best behavior."

Alice shot them both a perky little grin and closed the door behind her.

After she was gone, Jonas swung his gaze to Robin. He nearly chuckled at her tight, closed-off body language. The grim countenance on her face, the disapproval in her eyes, the austere set of her mouth. She was the perfect example of the frustrated female, and it was killing him not to make a comment that would bring that fact to her attention.

She opened her mouth to speak, and he dutifully remained silent, gladly handing her the shovel to dig her own grave.

"First," she stated flatly, "I want to make it perfectly clear my job has nothing whatsoever to do with my *thinking* of signing over my rights to Tony. I could call the magazine tomorrow and they'd give me a position where I didn't have to travel." She hesitated, then leaned forward a fraction of an inch as she continued. "I was expecting your parents, Jonas. I was thinking that I'd give them total custody, because...because..."

Because I know next to nothing about raising children, she wanted to say. But she clamped her lips shut, unable to bring herself to unburden herself to someone who would only use the information against her in some sneering joke. She didn't see any reason to reveal to him her most personal reasons for her actions. She owed Jonas Winslow no excuses. He deserved none.

She inhaled deeply and leaned even closer to him. "I was expecting Sara and Jeff to name at least one, maybe two, mature, responsible adults—"

"Wait a minute." He lifted his hand, palm side out. "There's no need to insult me."

But he really wasn't too offended by her words. She'd let him know a long time ago how she felt about him. He was more interested in the information she'd disclosed about her job.

"I'm sorry," she begrudgingly allowed. "I don't want to fight."

Jonas's mind churned. Since his sister hadn't named Amy as guardian, it looked as if his plans to get her to help him with the baby—at least for the time it took him to create new material for his new book—were going to fall through. If he could get Robin to agree to stick around for a few months... A hastily thought-out plan began to form in his head.

Robin straightened her back and crossed her arms again. She hadn't meant to hurt Jonas's feelings. But at the same time, she had to be honest with the man. This was no time to become tongue-tied or flustered. She simply had to put her feelings on the line.

"To tell you the truth," she said, "my finding out that you're the other guardian changes everything. I can't in good conscience allow you to raise my brother's baby. Just look at you." She pointed at him. "You're a mess. It looks like your hair hasn't been cut in months. Your shirt cuff is frayed." Her gaze traveled down the length of him. "You probably have holes in your socks."

At that moment, the silence of the tiny office was interrupted by a loud grumbling sound emanating from his stomach.

"And you probably haven't eaten today, either."

Hearing no rebuttal from him, Robin was overtaken with a sudden boldness that surprised her. She looked him in the eye. "And I haven't even mentioned the fact that you never take anything seriously. You live your whole life making a big joke out of everything. I can't allow you to influence Tony with your weird, one-sided, chauvinistic views."

She expected him to explode in anger, to jump up from his chair, to pace the room, to tell her off, to yell and shout. But he did none of those things.

His green gaze was calm as he suggested, "We could do it together."

The words stunned her. "Do what together?"

"Take care of Tony," he said.

She had only discovered a few minutes ago that, for some reason, Sara's parents couldn't take Tony. And she was only just beginning to contemplate the problems involved in raising the baby herself. The idea of spending even a short period of time with Jonas—let alone the years and years it would take until her nephew was grown— scared the bejesus out of her. She couldn't even think about it.

"Where are your parents, Jonas?" The question came out sounding like a lamentation.

The corners of his mouth drew down. "They've retired to Florida. My father had a stroke six months ago. He was left partially paralyzed. His mind isn't all that clear anymore, either."

"I'm so sorry," she said. "I didn't know."

"Mom spends all her time caring for him."

"Oh." The tiny exclamation left her in a breathy whisper. Hearing about Jonas's parents' plight brought back vivid memories of her own parents, and the reason she'd been determined all her life to be independent.

Jonas reached up to rub his neck, and Robin noticed how his coffee-colored hair fell down over the back of his hand. She'd chastised him about its length just moments ago, but now she found herself wanting to touch the silky locks, to stroke her fingers along the warm skin of his neck—in an effort to console him, of course.

He stared at her. "We could do it, Robin."

"No...I'm not sure..." She shook her head dubiously. "I really don't feel that we—"

"It wouldn't have to be forever." He placed the palms of his hands flat on the arms of the chair. "We could do it for say...eight or ten months. By then, we'd know each other better. We'd know which one of us is more capable of raising Tony."

"I don't know." Her words came slowly and were definite evidence of her uncertainty. There was so much they hadn't talked about, so many things that needed to be discussed. But she found herself saying, "Eight or ten months?"

"Mmm-hmm," he said, smiling. "We could handle that, couldn't we?"

He was being so nice, she thought, so different. *So charming.* Almost as though he was up to something—

Just then the door was pushed open, nudging into Jonas's chair. He hopped up and pulled open the door and a tall, chubby blonde walked into the small office. On her hip was perched a toddler with flame-red curls atop his head. The baby grinned and clapped gleefully at the sight of Jonas.

"Unka, Unka," he called.

"Tony!" Jonas took the child from the woman. "How ya doing, big guy? Hi there, Amy."

The woman nodded bashfully. "Sorry I'm late. Tony fell asleep during the service, so I took him home for a nap and he just woke up not too long ago."

"That's okay," Jonas told her.

"I had no idea what you were talking about this morning," she said. "I wasn't sure what meeting you meant. I just figured you needed me to bring Tony down here."

Robin listened to the two of them as Jonas tried to explain the misunderstanding. Evidently he had thought that this woman was going to be named as Tony's guardian. Their conversation became muffled as Robin focused on her nephew.

Tony was beautiful! Robin hadn't seen him since he was about six weeks old. The boy was the spitting image of her brother, Jeff, and Robin felt tears spring to her eyes.

"I'd like you to meet Robin Hampstead," she heard Jonas say. "Robin, this is Amy Lane. She was Sara's best friend, and she's been keeping an eye on Tony for the past . . . few days."

"Nice to meet you," Robin said.

Again, Amy's nod was bashful, her blond hair falling into her eyes. She looked up at Jonas. "Listen, I really have to go. I left the kids in the car with Ray and it won't take long for them to drive him stark raving mad."

Jonas chuckled. "Sure. And thanks again for everything, Amy." He closed the door behind her.

"Hey there, Tony," Robin said.

The baby laughed.

"You want to come to Aunt Robin?"

Tony leaned into Jonas's shoulder and plunked his tiny thumb in his mouth.

"It's all right," Jonas assured her. "He'll get to know you quickly."

Alice came into the office. "Well, did we get everything worked out?"

She scooted around Jonas and sat behind her desk. Jonas sat back down and placed the baby on his knee.

"We think so," he said.

Looking at Robin, Alice asked, "You're going to sign over rights?"

"Oh, no," Jonas said in a rush. "We're going to do this. Together."

He smiled at Robin for confirmation and she made a valiant effort to smile back, but her lips felt trembly. How could he be so bright and chipper about this sudden turn of events? She was having difficulty dealing with the way her plans kept bending and twisting with such unpredictability. She wasn't at all certain this was the right thing to do.

Alice heaved a sigh. "Then we do have a problem, because the judge won't appoint you both. I mean, she would have if you were married to each other, but... There will be money issues to be addressed, and decisions about the child's welfare. His schooling and such. What if the two of you didn't agree?" She shrugged. "Whose opinion would, or should, hold more weight?"

Robin didn't know whether to feel disappointed or elated. But Jonas's frustration was as clear as the frown knitting his brow.

Alice was shaking her head as she eased back into her chair. "It's just too bad you two aren't married."

Sensing Jonas's mischievous gaze on her, Robin swiveled her head in his direction.

"Oh, no," she said after seeing the blatant message in his twinkling green eyes. "Don't you look at me like that."

Chapter Two

"That was the tackiest wedding I've ever attended." Robin crossed her arms over her chest and stared out the small, square-shaped window of the plane, but the inky blackness of night kept her from seeing anything. She'd spent so much of her time over the past two days traveling in the air, that she was becoming accustomed to the constant ringing in her ears from the vibration of the huge jet engines.

"Hey," Jonas said, pausing long enough to chuckle, "our nuptials may have been as tacky as a polyester leisure suit, but it solved my problem."

His choice of words hit her wrong and she swung her gaze in his direction.

"*Our* problem," he quickly amended.

Robin sighed. "But a drive-through wedding chapel?" she asked. "I felt like I was going to the bank."

Again, he laughed. "Fly to Vegas, deposit a fee and withdraw a marriage certificate. Pretty convenient."

She shook her head. "Pretty tacky," she muttered under her breath.

Suddenly Robin felt more tired than she'd ever felt in her life. Resting her elbow on the narrow window ledge, she closed her eyes and rubbed her fingers lightly across her forehead.

"You must be exhausted."

The teasing lilt in Jonas's voice was replaced with genuine concern.

"Why don't you lean your head back and take a nap?"

She nodded and tried to comply with his suggestion. So much had happened over the past two days. And there was something about traveling thousands of miles to attend a memorial service only to be whisked off once again to travel yet more thousands of miles to be wed that made a person just a little restless.

She couldn't believe everything that had happened to her. Just yesterday—or had it been the day before?—she'd been sitting in a plush hotel suite preparing notes for the article she was writing about restaurants in the Hawaiian tropics. Who would have thought that she'd become guardian of her fourteen-month-old nephew and wife to the child's uncle? It was ludicrous! Laughable! Or would have been laughable, if she were the type of person who found the twists and turns of fate a laughing matter.

A sigh escaped her. Jonas was just such a person. *I'll bet he's dying to let loose an uproarious guffaw,* she thought. And she was certain he would do just that before all this was over.

Mrs. Jonas Winslow! This whole business was so... weird.

But what else could she have done? she asked herself. She couldn't have let him raise Tony. No way! She couldn't have allowed that to happen.

No, she'd simply stick to Jonas's plan; remain his wife for eight months, ten at the most, he'd said, and in that time she'd take a crash course in baby rearing. With Jonas there to give what help he could, Robin was a little more confident that she could learn the basics. She felt the tiniest twinge of guilt about using him this way—for using him was exactly what she was doing. Because she would never, ever agree to give him full custody of Tony. Her future might be a little fuzzy and out of focus right now regarding her career and where she and Tony would finally make their home, but she had plenty of time to work out all those details.

Sleep eluded her, and there was nothing to read except the complimentary magazine published by the airline. The only thing left to do was talk.

"Will we be picking Tony up when we get in?" she asked Jonas.

"I think we should. I mean, Amy has had Tony for...let's see...at least five days now." He absently rubbed the back of his neck. "You see, Amy was babysitting for Jeff and Sara when they...left for their long weekend in the mountains."

She lifted her head and focused on Jonas's clear, green gaze. "What happened to them, Jonas?" she asked, the words barely a whisper. "What happened to Jeff and Sara?"

There was anguish in his green gaze when he looked at her. "Carbon monoxide poisoning," he told her. "The cabin they were renting had a gas furnace—a gas furnace that hadn't been cleaned properly. Spring nights in the Allegheny Mountains can get a little chilly." His eyes shifted to the small window. "Either Sara or Jeff turned up the heat before they went to bed." He cleared his throat and focused on her face as he finished, "And they didn't wake up."

Sadness swelled in her throat and her eyes prickled with emotion. Who would have thought that the purely innocent act of turning the thermostat dial could kill Jeff and Sara, two people who were—

Who were what? she wondered. At today's memorial service she'd made the painful discovery that she didn't know her brother and his wife. Didn't know them at all.

The yawning emptiness that had threatened her so fiercely this afternoon at the church now returned with a vengeance.

She'd thought she'd pushed it aside, buried it along with her grief, until she could take care of the meeting at family court. Then that meeting had gone haywire and here she was on an airplane with a thin gold band around the third finger of her left hand. The turmoil of the day had helped her to forget the hollowness inside her that should have been filled with warm, happy memories of growing up with Jeff, glittering reminiscences of her brother, his wife and his baby son. But she had none. There was nothing to fill the ugly void inside her. And the barren feeling grew.

Robin felt the overwhelming urge to flee. As she did this afternoon when she'd left the service to walk in the rain until she'd found the small coffee shop. But in the close confines of the airplane, there was no place for her to go.

Squeezing her eyelids shut, she felt hot tears slip silently down her face.

"Oh, Robin." Jonas's rich voice was a near whisper. "They didn't suffer."

He slid his hand over hers. The warmth of his skin gave her more comfort than she'd ever dreamed was possible. His touch seemed to chase away the hated empty feeling in her chest.

Almost of their own volition, her fingers tightened their grip on his. She didn't want to, but she needed to use this man as a lanyard to tranquillity until she could regain her composure.

She could never tell him what she was feeling—reveal to him the black, gaping hole inside her. He would never understand. In fact, he'd most probably laugh or jeer at her vulnerability just as he'd done at little Tony's christening.

No, she could never let on how she was hurting. But his presence alone helped her. The warm solidness of him somehow made her feel less susceptible to the threatening emptiness.

With a gentleness that nearly took away her breath, Jonas smoothed his other hand along her forearm. Heat penetrated the thin cotton fabric of her sleeve and radiated in concentric waves up her arm.

The void diminished, smaller and smaller, until it was a dark pinpoint that she could easily push to the back of her brain. Jonas had rescued her from falling headlong into the terrible cavern of…of… She wasn't able to put a name to it. Didn't want to dwell on the horrible feeling long enough to do so. But Jonas had saved her from it. Without even knowing he'd done anything.

She sniffed, smoothed away the tear track that trailed down her cheek and gave him a small smile. "I'm glad to know that, Jonas. Thank you."

"And I've already contacted my lawyer about suing the owners of the cabin." His gaze turned suddenly ruthless. "When I finish with them, Tony will want for nothing."

"Except a mother and father." The bitter aside slipped from her lips before she could stop it.

His mouth thinned as he nodded ruefully. "You're right," he said. "But you and I are going to do what we can. We're going to give Tony everything we're able to give." Then he added, "For as long as we're able to give it."

Robin inhaled slowly, deeply, somewhere in the pleasant hazy state between deep sleep and alert wakefulness. The scent that enveloped her was warm and woodsy, as if she was walking through a forest in the heat of summer. But in her groggy state, she noticed something else about the bosky aroma. Something different. Something her sluggish rationale couldn't quite define.

Her subconscious made a valiant effort to snuggle back into the comfort and security of slumber, and it nearly succeeded. But there was something strange about her pillow, the semiconscious part of her argued. Something about it needed to be duly noted, recognized. For her own good.

An audible, sleepy sigh escaped her lips as Robin made a lethargic effort to discover what it was her brain was warning her against. Twisting her head the tiniest bit, she settled into a warm, unbelievably comfortable niche beneath her cheek. Granted, the pillow wasn't as soft as what she was used to, but the heat radiating from it more than made up for downy softness. And there was something about the niche that wasn't right. But the scent was wonderful. Descriptive words floated languidly through her mind—heated...secure...arboreal...male. Male?

Robin dragged her eyelids open and leaned forward in an attempt to sit up, but a weight on her shoulder made it impossible.

She blinked, and very slowly, very carefully, she looked down. There snuggled firmly under her breast was a hand. Another was planted on the flat of her stomach. Hands that were not hers, her fuzzy brain reasoned. Male hands.

Her thinking was becoming clearer with each second that passed. Jonas's hands.

Heavens above! She was nestled in Jonas's arms like a wanton vixen. What in the world would he think?

She lay perfectly still, praying that he, too, had dropped off to sleep. Lifting her gaze so she could view his face, she saw that his eyes were closed, his breathing rhythmic and slow.

He was such a handsome man. Even with a day's growth of stubble darkening his jaw. Even with his coffee-colored hair untrimmed and hanging over the collar of his shirt.

His brows were as dark as the hair on his head and well formed over his eyes. His nose was straight. Not too big, nor too small, but just right. His cheekbones were strong, angular, as was his jawline. There were hollows in his cheeks such as those seen on models and health-food fanatics. But Robin was certain Jonas's hollows had nothing to do with eating health food, but the lack of eating altogether. She nearly chuckled with her next thought—Jonas needed taking care of just as much, if not more, than little Tony.

A warning bell went off in her head. Looking after Jonas was not part of her plan. Learning to care for her nephew was her top priority. And that's all she wanted to focus on.

But sleeping in his arms had been heaven!

The whispery opinion came from somewhere in the back of her brain. Well, she decided, that's where it will have to return. She couldn't afford to complicate an already difficult situation by becoming physically attracted to Jonas.

Noticing that her skirt had hitched up to show a healthy slice of her thigh, she stirred just enough so she could tug the material somewhat into place.

Jonas straightened in his seat, pulling his arms from around her. He stretched and covered his mouth as he yawned.

"I'm sorry," he said, his voice hoarse with sleep. "I must have dozed off."

Robin said a quick, silent thank-you to her guardian angel. He hadn't noticed how she'd snuggled close to him. Hadn't seen her bare leg.

"I'm sorry I woke you," she murmured, meaning every word with every fiber of her being.

He rubbed his hands over his face and raked his fingers through his shaggy hair.

"Oh, but I'm the one who's sorry."

His grin filled with the kind of mischief that naturally put a person on guard. Robin stopped smoothing the wrinkles out of her blouse and waited.

"I tried to stay awake," he said. "I was really enjoying the way you were clinging to me. Like a flea on a dog's back."

She glared. How could she ever have worried about being physically attracted to this man? All he had to do was open his mouth and he instantly dissolved any temptation she might have felt for him.

Yes, she had awoken to find herself resting against him. Okay, she admitted, she'd been cleaving to him. Like a wanton vixen, as she remembered silently describing herself. But it was utterly rude of him to liken her to a flea. On a dog's back, no less! Well, *he* was a dog. A low-down, dirty dog!

He should have been gentleman enough to not notice. Or, since he had, at least courteous enough not to mention the fact.

But what else should she have expected from him? *Nothing,* she told herself. *Absolutely nothing!*

She was fuming as the pilot announced the landing at Baltimore/Washington International Airport, fuming as she and Jonas grabbed their carry-on bags and departed the plane, fuming as they made their way out of the terminal building and to the auto park where Jonas had left his car. Jonas tried to talk to her, but she refused to explain her anger. Just because she'd married the man didn't mean she owed him any justification for what she did or how she felt.

The ride from the airport was made in silence except for the soft music playing on the radio.

As he parked the car in the driveway of Amy's house, he said, "Look, it's late. We're both tired. And we don't want to upset Tony by letting him see us arguing the first time we're all together."

"Who's arguing?" She opened the car door and stepped out onto the asphalt.

Jonas came around the car. "Let's talk about this, Robin. I know you're angry. But I haven't figured out why yet."

She stopped short and whirled on him. "And that only makes me angrier." She turned to stalk off, but he reached out and placed his hand on her shoulder.

"Wait a second," he said. "Just give me a minute, okay?"

Plunking her fist on her hip, she cocked her head and stared at him.

"You're mad because I looked at you while you were sleeping?"

The look on her face must have told him he'd hit the bull's-eye.

His mouth tilted in a smile. "Well, you *are* my wife."

Her gaze turned to a glower. She brushed his hand from her shoulder and stormed toward the house.

Jonas jogged to catch her. "Come on, Robin. I was only kidding."

"And that's what comes naturally to you, isn't it? To joke and laugh and ridicule."

"Please, just wait."

But she wouldn't be stopped.

"I didn't mean to hurt you," he said, skipping along beside her. "I didn't know you'd be offended by my looking at you."

It wasn't the fact that he'd looked that angered her. No, in fact she was kind of . . . flattered by the idea.

The thought stopped her dead in her tracks and Jonas nearly plowed into her.

She was *not* flattered by Jonas ogling her in her sleep! Where had that notion come from?

Without taking the time to answer the silly question, or ponder the silly thought of flattery, Robin got back to the original argument. It wasn't the fact that he'd looked that angered her, it was the fact that he'd thrown it up in her face, joked about it and how she'd cuddled up to him. She'd been asleep, for heaven's sake. How could she have known she was using him as a human pillow?

However, what had hurt her the most was the fact that he'd compared her to an insect—an icky, bloodsucking insect!

But she had no intention of telling him how she felt *or* what he'd done. No intention at all of discussing it further. To do so at this point would only make her more vulnerable to his black, vicious humor.

"Look," she told him, "let's just drop the whole issue. We need to collect Tony and get him home into his own bed."

"So you're not angry with me anymore?"

"I said I'd drop it, didn't I?"

One dark brow rose as he said pointedly, "You didn't answer my question."

"Jonas!" She actually growled.

"Okay, okay. Let's get the baby."

Even though it was quite late, Amy was still awake and waiting for them. Sara's best friend hadn't been so sure that Jonas and Robin flying off to Nevada to get married was the best solution, but she wished them the best of luck and told them to call if they ran into any problems with Tony.

Once they arrived at Jeff and Sara's home, Robin accepted Jonas's offer to get up with the baby should he awaken in the night. She knew he'd offered as a way to assuage the animosity she was feeling toward him, but she accepted nonetheless. After the past two days of seesawing emotions and flying back and forth across the country, she could use a good night's sleep. In exchange, he'd asked if she would mind watching Tony during the morning hours so he could get some work done. She'd agreed, knowing that the few phone calls she needed to make to her employers at *Fancy Food* could be made in just a few moments while Tony napped.

Having slept soundly through the night, she awoke to the sounds of chirping birds in the tree by her window and the smell of freshly brewed coffee.

She slipped into her white knit robe and tied the sash as she went down the stairs toward the kitchen.

Jeff and Sara had chosen a beautiful house. Robin had stayed here for a few days when the baby had been christened. The traditional colonial design had spacious rooms, yet it also had some interesting nooks and crannies. Jonas had told her yesterday that, upon Jeff's death, the house had been paid for through an insured mortgage. So, she and Jonas had agreed that they should live in the house together—in separate bedrooms, of course—so that Tony would have as normal surroundings as possible.

Robin entered the big, eat-in kitchen with its terra-cotta tiled floor and tastefully papered walls, opened the cabinet and pulled out a sky blue mug.

After filling the mug with hot, steaming coffee, Robin leaned against the counter and sipped. She cradled the warm ceramic between her palms and looked around the kitchen. Sara had done a wonderful job of making this room inviting. This was Sara's kitchen and she'd never spend another moment in it. She'd never again use the gleaming mixer, the huge microwave, the state-of-the-art coffee grinder...

I don't want to feel sad today, Robin thought. And pushing herself away from the countertop, she went in search of Jonas and Tony.

She found Jonas in Jeff's office. He was sitting at the desk, totally immersed in the article he was editing. Again she was taken aback by how handsome he was. The rich brown color of his hair gleamed in the sunlight pouring through the window. His broad shoulders—

Don't do this, she scolded. But her eyes continued to feast on him. And, shockingly, her heart began to race.

"Good morning," she called softly, knowing that alerting him to her presence was the only way to tame these raging hormones she never knew she had. She needed to make him talk, needed to allow him to make himself look like a jerk, and she could do it just by engaging him in normal conversation.

"Well, hello there," he said. "You look well rested this morning."

His smile seemed free of inference, almost charming. But Robin was on her guard.

"Is there some reason why I shouldn't?" she asked. "Are you angry that you had to get up with Tony?"

Bewilderment crossed his brow. "I'm not angry. In fact, Tony slept through the night."

"Oh," she said, hearing the disappointment in her voice. Not that the baby had slept soundly, but that Jonas's initial greeting hadn't held any hidden umbrage and she was left looking grumpy.

Jonas must have heard the frustration in her tone because his brows rose and he said, "I got a good night's sleep, too. Does that mean our deal is off?"

"What are you talking about?"

"Are you going to watch Tony this morning so I can get some work done?"

"Of course I am." A lock of her curly hair had fallen into her eyes and she brushed at it. "Just because you didn't need to get up with him doesn't mean you wouldn't have, right? So our deal stands as made."

"Good," he said, "because I do my best work in the morning."

She grinned. "And I take a while to warm up to it."

One of his dark brows rose. "You'll be working?"

"I do have a career," she said lightly. "I have an article that needs finishing. And I thought I'd call the magazine to see if they could give me some position I can fill from here."

When he didn't respond immediately, she was impelled to ask, "Do you have a problem with that?"

"Of course not." He laid down his drawing pencil. "So I'll work mornings and you'll work afternoons. Is that feasible?"

She nodded. His last question was almost terse. As though he hadn't expected her to continue with the magazine. Realization struck; he'd thought she would quit her job outright to take care of Tony. Was he out of his mind?

But she didn't want to fight with him. He'd agreed to a work schedule, that's all that was important for the time being.

"Well, where is he?" She kept her tone pleasant, hoping to keep the conversation on the right track.

"Still sleeping," he said, his tone still edged with hardness. But his words softened as he continued. "I guess the little guy has been through a lot in the past few days."

"Yeah," she agreed. "Poor thing's going to have a rough time of it."

Jonas nodded solemnly.

"I thought I might take him out today," she said. "If you'll point the way to the park, we'll get out of your hair for a while. Maybe I'll check the pantry and stop off at the grocery store on our way home."

"Sounds good."

"Mama. Mama. *Maaaaaama.*"

The monitor on the kitchen counter magnified Tony's voice as clear as day. Robin smiled.

"Sounds like he's awake," she said. "I'll go bring him down for some breakfast. You go ahead with your work."

She hurried up the stairs and down the hall. The door of the baby's room was ajar and she pushed it open and went inside.

Robin smiled brightly. "Good morning!"

Tony froze in his crib, his wide brown eyes filling with fear.

If she'd stopped to think, she'd have realized that she should never have approached the crib. But she was so intent on calming the baby's anxiety that she didn't think, she simply acted.

Tony didn't move a muscle until she reached the crib railing. When she held out her hands to him, he began to scream as though she were an evil, ugly troll. Tony scrambled to the far corner of his bed, even though she crooned reassuring words to him.

"Here, here, now." Jonas rushed into the room. "What's all this?"

"Unka," Tony sobbed, huge crocodile tears spilling from his eyes.

Robin stepped away from the crib so Jonas could scoop up Tony. The baby buried his face in his uncle's neck.

The rejection and hurt she felt swelled in her throat until it became a hard, painful knot.

"He doesn't like me." She forced the whispered words around the lump. Hot tears burned her eyes.

"Come on, now," Jonas said, reaching out with his free hand to touch her arm. "It's not that he doesn't *like* you." His tone was soft and soothing. "He doesn't *know* you."

The rational part of her mind took in Jonas's explanation, even agreed with it, but the emotional part of her brain still felt bruised by Tony's shunning of her.

"We should have thought about this," Jonas said. "Seeing how he was a little shy of you at the courthouse."

Robin felt numb as she nodded.

"Let's just stick together for a few days," he suggested. "I'll put off working until Tony's as comfortable with you as he is with me."

What a nice thing for him to suggest. Warm blood rushed through her veins, bringing back her sense of feeling with tingling clarity. Gratitude welled within her, and she wanted to reach up on her tiptoes and kiss him on the cheek.

But she hesitated as a dark, silent voice whispered inside her. *He's not putting off his work for you, you idiot. He's doing it for the baby.*

"Of course," she murmured to herself.

"So, you think it's a good idea?" he asked.

"What? Oh, yes," she said. "And I'll put off working for a while, too. It shouldn't take too long, do you think?"

"Nah," Jonas said with a smile. "A couple days at the most."

Even as she said, "Okay," Robin battled with her mixed feelings about spending the next few days in close proximity to Jonas. She'd thought they would take turns being with little Tony, and now it was necessary that the three of them be thrown together for all activities. The idea made her uncomfortable for some reason, made her feel unsafe.

She wasn't afraid of Jonas; it wasn't that at all. It was just that he threatened her... security. No, that wasn't it, either.

Why, then, she wondered, did she balk at the thought of spending time with him?

Before she could ponder the question further, Tony began to make deep, grunting noises. She and Jonas looked at each other in surprise. The baby lifted his head to stare intently into his uncle's eyes. His precious little face turned beet red as he strained, and immediately following, there was a loud, stinky explosion in his diaper.

Jonas looked at her, trying hard to contain his mirth. "I guess it's time for me to change the lad's pants," he said.

A snicker escaped her throat. "You *are* the favored one," she replied.

Chapter Three

Robin rummaged in the kitchen pantry trying to find something to feed Tony for breakfast while Jonas was busy changing the toddler's diaper and dressing him for the day. She smiled as she heard Jonas's voice coming over the baby monitor. He was talking his way through the diaper change, evidently having forgotten that Robin could eavesdrop on his every word.

"Okay," she heard Jonas say, "the bottom is clean." Then he added, "Tony, let's remember to pick up more baby wipes at the store."

A grin tugged at the corners of Robin's mouth. She went to the desk in the corner of the kitchen and started a grocery list, placing baby wipes at the very top.

"Okay, diapers," he said. "Where are the diapers?"

There was a scrambling sound that had Robin chuckling.

"No, Tony, keep still now. Uncle Jonas is moving as fast as he can. You have to be patient."

"Toy," Tony demanded.

"You want the teddy bear?"

"No." The baby's tone was firm, decisive. "Toy."

With her ear glued to the monitor, Robin leaned against the counter, all thoughts of breakfast pushed from her mind.

"Here," she heard Jonas offer, "how about these keys? They're pretty colors. Red. Blue. Green. Look at this yellow one." Another scrambling sound and then she heard the plastic keys bounce off the changing table. "No, no, Tony. Lay still for Uncle Jonas."

Tony whined.

"Okay, let's go over to the toy chest and you pick out what you want."

The surrender in Jonas's heavy sigh had Robin pressing her fingers against her lips to hold back the mirth that bubbled from within her. She listened as the two of them moved across Tony's bedroom and began digging in the chest full of cars, trucks, plastic balls, airplanes and stuffed animals. Jonas offered each toy to the child and Tony rejected each one.

Robin found herself completely caught up in the entertainment their conversation brought her. She looked forward to the day when she and her nephew could communicate in the same easy manner. She hoped it wouldn't take Tony too long to learn to trust her as he obviously trusted Jonas.

"So you want the duck," she finally heard Jonas say. "Why didn't you say so?"

"Duck," Tony proclaimed triumphantly.

The deep rich sound of Jonas's chuckle sent shivers coursing along Robin's spine. He had such a nice voice. And he was so calm and patient when dealing with Tony. Maybe her brother, Jeff, and his wife knew exactly what they were doing when they'd named Jonas as Tony's guardian.

Her eyes grew wide, the thought startling her so that she took a staggering step away from the counter—away from the monitor where Jonas's voice floated out over the air.

She could be calm and patient with the baby. She knew she could. She only needed to be given the chance. She only needed to gain Tony's trust.

Suddenly she relived the rejection she'd felt only minutes before when her nephew had cried as she'd entered his room. But luckily she was able to stave off the emotional onslaught and view the scene in her mind from a more analytical point of view.

Jonas had been right. Tony had been frightened of her, not because he disliked her, but because he didn't know her well enough to feel safe and secure in her presence.

Well, Robin thought, she'd put the baby at ease. She'd let him know that she could be counted on. She'd learn to care for him so that he'd know he could depend on her....

Her intake of breath was sharp as a realization struck her with full force—she *wanted* Tony to depend on her. She'd never wanted anything so much in her life. The feeling was so strange to her. All her life she'd run from one end of the world to another in an effort to keep herself free and independent. She'd never wanted to have anyone rely on her. Years of seeing her mother slave for her severely ill father had implanted in her a fierce desire for freedom and independence.

But why the change of heart now? she wondered.

"Oh, Tony!"

Jonas's loud exclamation jerked Robin from her thoughts. The baby began to cry and she wondered if she should run upstairs to see what happened or if she could help.

"It's okay," she heard Jonas soothe. "Don't cry. Let's just get a diaper on and we'll go down to breakfast. Aunt Robin is fixing you something good to eat. Let's worry about getting you dressed later."

At the mention of food, Robin's gaze swept across the immaculate kitchen, the clear table, the spotless counters. She hadn't even started to prepare anything for Tony to eat. Scurrying to the pantry, she pulled out a round box of oatmeal and began reading the instructions for preparation. She found a small bowl and a measuring cup. She bolted for the refrigerator and slowed down long enough to carefully pour out the right amount of milk. The microwave oven buttons beeped as she programmed in the proper time.

She searched the cabinets and found a bright blue plastic cup with a tight-fitting lid that Tony could sip from and placed it on the tray of the high chair along with a spoon.

"Put your leg down, Tony," Jonas said. "Here, here. No, lay still. Quit squirming now."

His light tone in his voice was forced now and Robin could actually feel his frustration. She would like to have enjoyed the hard time he was having diapering the baby, but she was in too much of a rush to stir the oatmeal and then fill the cup with chilled apple juice she'd found in the door of the fridge.

Robin was sprinkling brown sugar on the steaming oatmeal when she heard Jonas's footsteps coming down the stairs. She looked up when they entered the room.

"Hi, Tony." She kept her greeting bright and friendly. Her quick glance at Jonas had her eyes widening with curiosity. "What happened to you?" she asked.

He looked a little flustered, but there was mirth in his green gaze as he explained. "Tony had a little accident."

Jonas tugged his wet pant leg away from his body. "But I did learn a valuable lesson . . ."

Robin's mouth quirked up in a grin. "Don't let Tony run around without a diaper on?"

Jonas nodded solemnly and then joined in with her light laughter.

The sound emanating from deep in his chest was rich and vibrant and it did strange things to the pit of her stomach. Her smile slowly faded and she pressed her hand to her abdomen, but before she could rationalize her body's reaction to Jonas's glee, Tony began to chuckle, too.

Robin's attention suddenly riveted to the baby's face. She felt so relieved that he was happy.

"Oh," Jonas commented to Tony, "so you think what you did to Uncle Jonas was funny, huh?"

"Fun." The baby tried out the word, and he laughed again.

Jonas smiled at Robin, and again she felt her insides grow all quivery. She fought to keep her brow from wrinkling as she tried to figure out what was wrong with her. Was she coming down with the flu?

"I need to get a shower and change," Jonas told her. "But it'll have to wait until after we feed Tony."

The queer sensation she'd experienced when Jonas smiled at her was pushed aside by a new anxiety: she worried whether or not the baby would like the breakfast she'd prepared. It wasn't until that very moment that she realized she had no idea what fourteen-month-old toddlers ate in the morning. Would he like oatmeal? Did he have enough teeth to chew it? Should she have prepared some kind of baby cereal instead? Or mashed up some fruit? Could Tony digest fresh fruit?

Robin had realized all along she didn't know the first thing about rearing children, but the questions that flew through her brain, fast and furious, boggled the mind.

Jonas held Tony in one arm and moved into the center of the kitchen. The baby's happy countenance faded and apprehension filled his big, brown eyes with sudden fear as he glanced at Robin. It was almost as if he'd forgotten about his frightening experience upon awakening and was just now remembering.

His little chin quivered and the corners of his mouth tipped down. The sight filled Robin with a compassion the likes of which she'd never before felt. She wanted to wipe away all his anxiety, but that was a pretty difficult task when it was *her* that he feared.

"Oh, Tony," she crooned, "it's okay. Please don't be afraid of me."

She said the words but she didn't move, didn't dare take a step toward the child. She'd already seen the results of approaching him when he felt scared.

"Now, Tony," Jonas said. "This is Aunt Robin."

Tony slipped his thumb into his mouth, looked from Jonas to Robin and back to Jonas. The panic in his gaze broke Robin's heart and made her want to reach out to him. But she didn't. She simply waited for him to respond.

He twisted in Jonas's arms, turning his back to her and holding himself in that stiff position. His reaction couldn't have been more clear—he didn't want to deal with the situation. He didn't want to face what was happening, and in his child's mind he'd decided that ignoring Robin would make her go away.

But he had to face it. He had to deal with it. Because Robin wasn't going away.

Jonas looked at Robin and she read questions in his troubled, emerald eyes. *So what do we do?* he silently asked. *How do we fix this?*

She shrugged, feeling helpless and empty inside.

It was Jonas who took action. He approached Robin with Tony still in his arms, and he smoothed his strong, tanned hand up and down the toddler's back as he said, "Tony, Aunt Robin is a nice lady. She fixed your breakfast. She cooked oatmeal just for you."

Jonas was standing so close now that she could have reached out and touched his arm. Tony didn't move to acknowledge her in any way.

Jonas moved closer.

"Turn around, Tony." His tone was gentle but firm.

Robin felt her stomach grow jittery. She didn't want to force her nephew to accept her, but she knew it was in his best interest that he understand the circumstances as much as he could and come to terms with his present situation.

She was part of his present situation. The sooner he learned that, the better.

"Tony, turn around," Jonas repeated. "I want you to meet your aunt Robin."

Ever so slowly, Tony pivoted first his head, then his whole body, until he was facing Robin. Again the anxiety in his face, in his gaze, nearly killed her.

"It's okay, honey," she said softly. "I know you're afraid. But you don't need to be. I love you."

His fear seemed to lessen a tiny degree.

She reached out and touched his cheek.

Tony's eyes glistened with sudden tears.

Robin lowered her hand to her side.

"Now, look," Jonas said, his unwavering voice was balanced with just the right softness to get the baby's attention. "Aunt Robin is going to be here with us, Tony."

Then Jonas did the most astounding thing—he draped his free arm over her shoulders.

"I like Aunt Robin," he proclaimed. "And I know you're going to like her, too."

Robin felt blanketed in the male warmth emanating from Jonas. She could feel the heat of his arm penetrating the thin cotton fabric of her housecoat. There was a tiny, sensitive pulsing right at the back of her neck where his bare skin touched hers. It felt hot enough to make her want to flinch, but she fought the urge to do so.

A nice, woodsy aroma wafted around her and she inhaled deeply. Her heart pitter-pattered in her chest. She was enjoying his closeness too much, and just as she was about to chastise herself, she smelled something else...a light and fresh fragrance. Baby powder. She smelled baby powder.

Darting a quick glance at Jonas's hand where it dangled from her shoulder, she saw a pale white film of powder on his palm.

Mixing the dark, woodsy scent of cologne with baby powder didn't bring to mind the idea of a sensual aroma, and Robin was totally surprised when she found the smell quite sexy. So sexy, in fact, that her mouth pulled back in a grin she wasn't able to suppress.

Helplessly she looked up into Jonas's face and felt an immense relief to find his attention focused on Tony. She turned her gaze on little Tony and saw that he was studying her. She let her grin broaden into a full-fledged smile. It mattered not one whit that her smile had been caused by her reaction to Jonas's nearness—it only mattered that a smile was what her nephew needed to see from her right now.

The corners of Tony's mouth tipped up timidly.

"There it is," Jonas said. "Let's see that smile grow bigger and bigger."

His arm muscle contracted, pulling her even closer to him, and before she knew what was happening, she felt Jonas's firm, warm lips on her lower jaw. The kiss was over before she could blink, but her reaction to it lingered. Heat suffused her face and her whole body broke out in feverish, prickly tremors.

Robin swallowed and tried to keep the smile from sliding from her lips. She reached around behind her and grasped the edge of the counter for support.

"Robin is my friend," Jonas told Tony. "Robin is your friend, too."

He's lying. The thought soared through her head like a runaway asteroid.

She knew he was telling bald-faced lies. He really didn't think she was nice. He really didn't think of her as a friend. He was only trying to win Tony's trust. But the weight of his arm slung across her shoulder, the sound of his voice when he complimented her, the feel of his heartbeat where her skin was pressed against his chest were making her insides jitter with an undercurrent of...

No words would come to describe what she was feeling by being so near to Jonas, by feeling the warmth of him, by hearing his voice.

"Do you want to give Aunt Robin a kiss?" Jonas asked Tony.

The toddler's smile faded.

Robin shrugged out of Jonas's embrace. "I appreciate what you're doing, Jonas," she said. "But don't push it. He'll come around." To Tony, she said, "How about some breakfast?"

Tony looked into his uncle's eyes. "Eat," he demanded.

Jonas and Robin worked together to loosen the tray from the high chair. By the time the two of them had secured Tony in the seat, the child was losing all patience.

"Juice, juice." He pointed to the blue plastic sippy cup.

Robin set the cup on the tray and Tony promptly picked it up and took a long drink.

She stood near the high chair, the bowl of oatmeal in hand.

"Can he feed himself?" she asked Jonas.

He blinked several times. Finally he admitted, "I have no idea."

"Tony. Eat." The toddler slapped his hand on the wide expanse of the white plastic tray and the spoon clattered loudly.

Robin shrugged. "We'll just have to find out. Here goes nothing."

She set down the bowl in front of him.

Tony picked up the spoon and awkwardly dipped into the oatmeal. Robin couldn't help but chuckle as her nephew tried to fit the rounded edge of the spoon into his mouth. Oatmeal smeared over his upper lip and fell with a plop back into the bowl.

Meaning to help him guide the second scoopful into his mouth, Robin took his little hand in hers.

"Me do," Tony said. "Me do."

"Okay," Robin said softly. But he did allow her to help him with one bite before he shook off her grasp.

He played happily in the oatmeal, getting more of the sticky cereal on his face than in his stomach. And about every third spoonful, Robin gave him a little help.

She noticed Jonas's intoxicating scent before she heard his voice as he bent close to her ear to whisper, "You're doing great. If I can slip off without him noticing, I'm going to go shower and change."

Robin nodded.

It pleased her to see that she and her nephew had formed what she hoped could be called the beginnings of a relationship, albeit fragile. And she knew very well that Tony's hunger was the main reason he'd lost himself in the task of eating to the point that he'd forgotten to be afraid of her.

She realized that Jonas had left her alone, and she made an extra-special effort to engage Tony's attention so he wouldn't notice his uncle was gone.

Dropping the spoon onto the tray of the high chair, Tony picked up the blue cup in both his sticky hands and took a swig of apple juice.

Robin gazed at her nephew's headful of curly red hair. Unable to help herself, she reached out and fingered one silky, tightly curled lock. With his fiery hair and big brown eyes, Tony looked so much like his father.

Jeff had hated his unruly curls. Robin had been so much younger than her brother. She'd still been in elementary school when he'd started high school, but she remembered how the teenage girls had called the house every night for her brother. Robin's mother used to tease him that all those girls were in love with his curly red hair.

A memory! She remembered how her brother had felt about his curly hair. A wave of elation washed over her. Robin closed her eyes and envisioned how Jeff had flushed a deep red when his mother had joked with him about his girlfriends.

If there was one memory in her brain that could help fill that deep, wide void inside her, there must be others. There must be!

But as Robin absently helped little Tony spoon a scoop of oatmeal into his mouth, she couldn't come up with anything. The sound of her brother's voice. His favorite color. What foods he liked to eat. She couldn't even remember what his room had looked like.

Suddenly the black hole inside her seemed as empty as ever. She sighed and fought to focus on the here and now, rather than the past. Too late, she noticed that because she hadn't been talking to Tony, the child had lost interest in his breakfast and was gazing around the kitchen.

"Here, Tony," she said, hoping to regain his attention and keep him from noticing Jonas's absence. "Would you like another bite? It's good."

She loaded the spoon with oatmeal and waved it in front of Tony's eyes. When that ploy failed to work, she made amateur airplane noises by pursing her lips and exhaling through them.

Robin expected her nephew to laugh, or at least smile at her. But Tony did neither of those things. A moment of curiosity crossed his features, however, the emotion passed quickly and he simply stared at her as though she'd grown another nose. Then, he craned his neck to look behind him.

"Look, Tony," she said, her tone louder. "Look at Aunt Robin."

He ignored her.

"Unka?"

The fear in his little voice ripped through her like a jagged-edged knife. Yet she could hear the shower still running upstairs and knew that Jonas couldn't rescue her from the situation.

"It's okay." She tried to keep her tone as calm as possible, but the panic that rose in her throat made her efforts practically hopeless. "Please don't be afraid of me."

She reached out and touched Tony on the arm.

The high-pitched scream that lacerated the air nearly pierced her eardrum.

"Tony, Tony," she crooned. "Honey, please..."

Please what? she wondered. He was afraid of her. There was nothing she could say that would calm him. Nothing whatsoever.

Huge tears coursed down his cheeks as he sobbed. He twisted and pushed and strained to get out of the high chair, chanting, "Unka, Unka," in a heart-wrenching tone that made Robin's throat swell with emotion.

Her sight blurred as painful tears prickled her eyelids. She had to get this child to Jonas, shower or no shower. She couldn't allow Tony to feel afraid one moment longer than he had to.

Tears rolled down her face as she fumbled to unlock the tray from the chair.

"We'll go find Uncle Jonas," she told him. "We'll go right now."

Picking the toddler up, she had to turn her head as a fresh wave of shrieks bombarded her. She rushed out of the kitchen and down the hallway toward the steps that led upstairs, constantly murmuring reassurances she knew Tony wasn't interested in hearing.

She felt his moist, sticky palm press against her jaw as he attempted to escape her. But the oatmeal that coated his skin only caused his little hand to slide right off her face. The gooey residue he left behind felt cold and clammy, but Robin didn't have enough of her wits about her to wipe it off.

Tony kicked his feet and she grasped his thighs in a tight embrace, supporting his back with her free hand as she climbed up the long staircase.

Five more steps, she thought, aiming for the closed bathroom door as though it were an entrance to heaven itself. Four more steps. Three more. Two. One.

She pounded on the door, sobbing now almost as hard as the baby was.

"Let us in, Jonas!" she cried. "Tony needs you."

Her heart was pounding in her chest. Blood rushed through her ears like waves crashing on a storm-tossed beach. Tony's screams hadn't subsided one decibel and his little body trembled.

The water had stopped running and she banged on the door again.

"Jonas!"

"One second," he called. "What happened? Is he hurt?"

Jonas jerked open the door and Tony launched himself at his uncle.

"Whoa there, partner," Jonas said. "What's all this? He looks okay." He turned his questioning gaze on Robin. "With all the shouting and tears, I expected to at least see a little blood on the boy."

"It's all my fault." Robin could hardly speak, her throat was so constricted with emotion. "I got all wrapped up in thinking about how much Tony looks like Jeff, and I should have been keeping the baby busy so he wouldn't notice that you'd left the two of us alone—" she took a hiccupy inhalation "—he looked around for you and I couldn't get him to eat any more and I even tried to make an airplane but . . . but . . ."

"Here, here," Jonas said softly.

He pulled her to him with his free arm. Tony nestled against one of Jonas's shoulders and Robin melted into the other. He felt so good, so warm, so secure. Fresh tears gathered in her eyes and slipped down her cheeks. She felt them, cool against her skin in the heated air of the small room.

She listened to Jonas's voice, soothing and calm, as he consoled Tony. As he spoke to the baby, his hand trailed absently up and down her arm. He was sturdy and strong as she leaned against him, and she gratefully drank in every bit of comfort he gave.

The tension in the atmosphere diminished by degree until it was nearly imperceptible. Robin inhaled deeply and then exhaled the remaining anxiety from her body.

Finally she heard him say, "What am I going to do with you two?"

She heard a sucking sound and knew that Tony had found at least some of his security in his thumb. She'd found a great deal of consolation in the clean, soapy aroma wafting all around her.

"We're going to work this out."

Robin almost smiled as she realized Jonas's promise was as much for her as it was for little Tony.

"But I gotta tell you," he went on, "it's really not fair to actually pull me out of the shower dripping wet."

His chuckle rumbled deep in his chest, and Robin enjoyed the feel of it against the flat of her palm.

Her eyes flew open.

Yes, her hand was resting against his bare chest all right. The dark, springy hairs glistened with water droplets. She stepped away from him so fast that her heel struck the wicker wastebasket in the corner. It wobbled and then fell over on its side.

"I'm sorry," she said, unable to take her eyes off his broad chest, his muscular shoulders, still deliciously damp.

Ever so slowly, she raised her eyes. His sandy brown hair was tousled and soaking wet, fat drops of water from his shower ran down his face and neck. Her helpless gaze followed one particular water droplet on its slow, arduous trek down his chest, over a powerful pec, up and down definitely wavy abdominal muscles. She watched it narrowly escape the small trap his navel created. The bead of water collected strength as it captured other droplets that had been tangled in the curly hairs of Jonas's lower stomach.

Absently her tongue traveled slowly across her lips as the oval pearl gathered speed and then was soaked up by the fluffy terry-cloth towel secured around him. She blinked and then stared at the spot where the moisture had disappeared. Drawing her bottom lip between her teeth, she brazenly appraised the slice of muscular thigh disclosed by the too-small towel.

Robin swallowed, shocked by the rate at which her heart was pounding. She didn't even like this man. In fact, he had a way of irritating her, getting under her skin, as no one else could. Why then was she standing here gawking at him? Why was she experiencing these strange...desires?

No, she told herself. She did *not* desire Jonas. No way, no how.

She dragged her gaze back to his face. The smirk smeared across his face made her want to crawl into a corner somewhere and hide.

Here it comes, she thought. He's going to open his mouth and say something humiliating.

Jonas didn't disappoint her.

"You know, I think there's an old wives' tale that says if you stare at the opposite sex with that look in your eye—" his grin widened "—you just might go blind."

Chapter Four

That look in your eye... his words rang through her head like the irritating peal of a large, metallic bell. The fact that Jonas had witnessed her ogling him mortified her. And even worse, he'd recognized the... the hunger in her gaze caused by the sight of his nearly bare body. Dear Lord, she'd never live this down.

The wonderful, secure feeling Jonas had given her only seconds before melted under the heat of anger and embarrassment that roiled in her chest. Her eyes narrowed. Her teeth clenched tightly. Her shoulders stiffened until they became painful. She wanted to smack that smirk right off his face.

How could she ever, *ever* have found this man appealing?

She glared at him.

"What?" he said.

Her eyes narrowed even more. Her jaw jutted out in disgust.

Jonas laughed. "I was only joking, Robin. I was trying to lighten the mood."

Lighten the mood, indeed, she thought. His idea of lightening the mood was to humiliate the first person who came into view. He'd done it before, as she had been most personally aware.

She pressed her lips together, refusing to spit out the perfect rejoinder that would reveal just what she thought of him. She wanted desperately to put him in his place, but tension and fighting would only cause more anxiety in little Tony.

"Come on, Robin," Jonas said, lighthearted laughter still tinting his voice.

Tony chose that moment to chuckle merrily.

Her gaze darted to her nephew's face. The child still had tears in his eyes as a result of spending a few lousy minutes alone with her, but he was happy as he could be here in his uncle's arms.

Focusing her attention on Jonas's glittering green eyes, Robin felt her irritation bubbling up from inside her, nearly erupting in a rumble deep in her throat.

She turned and stormed out of the bathroom. The urge to slam her bedroom door was great, but she went to war with it and won.

Lord, but the man made her angry! She was shaking, inside and out.

Robin tore off her robe and tossed it across the unmade bed. She unbuttoned the soft, baggy shirt she used as a nightgown and jerked it from her shoulders.

"Lighten the mood," she muttered under her breath.

As she tugged on a pair of white leggings, a quiet voice inside her head whispered, *Well, Jonas did calm the baby down. And not only that, he made Tony laugh.*

"Oh, shut up," she grumbled and stuffed her head through the opening of the long, loose-fitting knit top. She pulled on slouchy green socks that matched her shirt and then slipped her feet into white canvas sneakers.

Sitting down on the edge of the mattress to tie her shoes, she felt totally exhausted.

The shower in the hallway bathroom turned back on, and Robin guessed that Jonas had taken Tony in with him. That was good because Tony needed cleaning up after all the oatmeal he'd plastered over his face and hands.

She sighed heavily and didn't seem to have the energy to get up off the bed. It was no wonder she was stressed out. She'd had not one, but two unnerving experiences with the baby this morning. Those alone would have been enough to dishearten anyone, but her emotions had continued the roller-coaster ride when she'd enjoyed a few happy moments feeding the baby, only to feel saddened with memories—or lack of them—of her brother, and then her blood pressure had careered at the sight of Jonas's naked chest. All of these things taken together were enough to fell a bull.

Robin sighed again. Maybe she'd overreacted to Jonas's comment. Maybe her emotions had been in such a turmoil that she'd been a tad irrational.

Nah, she firmly told herself. *No way.*

Even if his motives were pure and he'd only been trying to "lighten the mood," then he shouldn't have made it at her expense. He shouldn't have made her the butt of his joke.

Well, what else could she have expected from him? He'd done that exact same thing to her before at Tony's christening. He'd humiliated her in front of an entire roomful of people.

She'd simply have to protect herself from him in the future, that was all. She'd have to work hard to keep from doing anything he could taunt her about. The first thing she'd have to work on, she knew, was keeping her hormones in check.

Resting her chin in her palm, her elbow on her knee, Robin felt certain she could do just that. Anytime she felt the urge to admire Jonas's physique, she'd use her best defense—she'd just talk to him. He would be sure to snuff out any desire she might feel.

She felt better now that she had armed herself with a plan.

After running a brush through her short curls, Robin went downstairs, straight to the powder room off the main hallway. She rinsed the dried flakes of oatmeal and milk off her skin that Tony had smeared across her jaw, then went to the kitchen to clean up Tony's high-chair tray. That task accomplished, she poured herself a second cup of coffee and stepped out the back door into the bright sunshine.

The smell of spring was in the air. Early-blooming hyacinths and crocuses gave the air a heady fragrance. Tender leaf buds were blooming on the trees. The green of the leaves and the blazing purple, pinks and blues of the flowering bulbs were uplifting to Robin's spirit. She sat on the back porch, sipped her steaming coffee and let her soul soak up the goodness of the fresh air and sunshine.

"Bob-in."

The sound of Tony's high-pitched voice drew her gaze from the clouds trailing lazily across the sky. She turned and craned her neck up toward the back screen door but didn't see her nephew or Jonas.

"Say it again," Jonas said. "Louder."

"*Bob-in!*"

Robin's breath caught in her throat. Tony was saying her name. At least, he was trying to say it. She realized that the sound of the letter *r* must be hard for a baby to make.

"Here," she called, feeling overwhelmed with happiness.

She stood up and pulled open the back door. And there they stood. Jonas and Tony. Both of them with still-damp hair from their shower.

As she looked at her nephew, love filled her face with a wondrous smile.

"There's Aunt Robin." Jonas's voice was soft and calm.

Tony reached out and patted her cheek. "Bob-in," he said slowly. His dimples were defined when he smiled at her.

Robin thought her heart would burst with adoration.

"And where's Uncle Jonas?" Jonas asked.

The baby focused his attention on Jonas.

"Unka," Tony said, touching his uncle on the chin.

"And Tony?" This time it was Jonas's turn to grin as he playfully looked around him. "Where's Tony?"

"Tow-nee." Tony pointed to his own chest. "Tow-nee."

"Good boy," Robin said. "And you sure look spiffy in those green overalls. You match Aunt Robin. I'm wearing green, too."

She pointed to her green shirt and then to his corduroy overalls.

Tony's dark eyes lit up. He struggled in his uncle's arms and Jonas set him down on the floor. Tony toddled away from them, out through the kitchen and into the family room with the two adults following close behind him.

"He walks so well," Robin remarked.

"I remember," Jonas told her, "he was taking steps on his own at his birthday party two months ago." He lowered his voice to say, "Sara and Jeff were so proud of him."

They watched Tony dig into a huge wooden basket filled with toys.

A dark, dense cloud of regret descended on Robin. She wished so badly that she'd been around to attend Tony's first birthday party. She could easily imagine Sara lighting the candle on the brightly decorated cake, her brother with a video camera running as he taped it all, children laughing, singing. The dark despondency threatened to become overwhelming.

Robin pushed the emotion away from her as though it were a tangible thing. She'd had enough remorse, anger and rejection for one day. She refused to feel bad anymore.

"Ball," Tony declared, offering her the round, hollow toy.

She knelt down to be at his eye level.

"Geen ball."

"That's right." Robin couldn't keep the surprise from her voice. "You're such a smart boy."

"Geen," Tony repeated. Then he nodded with deep seriousness.

Robin looked up at Jonas. "He's smart." She straightened her knees and returned to a stand.

"Mine!"

She gazed down at the toddler and saw from the panic in his eyes that he thought she meant to keep his ball.

"Here you go," she said, handing it back to him. "He's really smart," she repeated to Jonas as Tony went back to the basket.

Jonas nodded. "Sara spent a lot of time with him."

"She didn't work?" Robin hated to ask, feeling embarrassed that she didn't know that simple piece of information about her sister-in-law.

"Sara worked at the mall part-time selling cosmetics before Tony was born," he told her. "But she wanted to be with Tony."

Robin nodded.

"Okay—" Jonas clapped his hands to get Tony's attention away from the toys "—who wants to go to the store? Does Tony want to go bye-byes?"

The baby laughed and ran to Jonas with his arms stretched out.

"I'd better grab a sweater for him," Robin suggested.

"And some diapers," Jonas said. "I think I saw a diaper bag sitting beside his changing table. Bring plenty of diapers. I used all the baby wipes."

"I put them on the grocery list," she told him. "You might want to put a few raisins in a container just in case he gets hungry."

"Good idea." He smiled. "See, we can do this."

As she ran up the steps toward the baby's room, she reminded herself yet again that she didn't even like this man. Why then, she wondered, was she reacting to him in such a purely physical manner? It seemed that all he had to do was look at her and her stomach churned with giddiness, her heart began to palpitate. She found the idea not only confusing but extremely irritating.

She snatched up the diaper bag and began loading it with diapers, baby powder and several little toys, trying hard all the while to vanquish the image of Jonas's smile from her mind.

Tony enjoyed the car ride to the local supermarket. He pointed to first one thing then another.

"Truck," he would say, or "cat," or "tree," or "sign," or "*big* truck."

Robin was impressed with his vocabulary.

"Sara must have spent a lot of time with him," she observed in a whisper.

Jonas only nodded.

She faced the front and forced herself to look out the window. Several times she'd caught herself staring at Jonas's profile. And even though she looked out at the town of Brenville, she could still picture how his sandy brown hair curled softly over the collar of his shirt. His nose was straight and just the right length for his strong-jawed face. His bottom lip was nice and full, and she wondered how it would feel on her own mouth . . .

"Stop," she muttered.

"What?"

"Nothing," she quickly answered Jonas's query.

"But—"

"Dog," Tony said.

"Where?" she asked, turning to see where Tony was pointing and desperate to put Jonas off.

She saw a woman walking with a leashed dog along the sidewalk. "That's right, Tony," Robin said. "That's a dog."

The baby made barking noises that had her chuckling.

Jonas steered the car into the large parking lot and killed the engine. "Here we are," he announced.

Tony gleefully clapped his hands.

They sat the baby in the seat of the metal cart, and with Jonas pushing, they entered the store.

Robin found out very quickly that Jonas was somewhat of a celebrity in the small town of Brenville. It seemed the three of them could barely move ahead three steps before someone stopped them to speak to Jonas.

Some of his fans agreed with the things he'd said in his column, and Robin had to suffer through seeing Jonas get all puffed up about something he wrote. But others disagreed with his opinions and they weren't afraid to let him know how they felt. Robin actually enjoyed listening to these exchanges.

Robin didn't make it a habit to read Jonas's syndicated column. In fact, she avoided it like the plague. She always disagreed with his opinion and reading his thoughts invariably made her angry, so she simply didn't.

One gentleman congratulated Jonas.

After they were far enough away so the man wouldn't overhear her, she asked, "What? Did you win some kind of award for your writing?"

"Nah," Jonas said, shrugging off her question.

And before she could inquire further, Tony became all excited.

"Candy," he shrieked. "Candy." Tony strained toward the gleaming, colorful bags hanging from hooks on the shelf.

"I don't know..." Robin looked at Jonas.

"Aww, what can it hurt?" Jonas said. "A little candy never hurt anybody."

"But don't you think we should buy him fresh fruit to snack on?" She lifted one hand. "Or crackers even? Something more nourishing than candy."

Jonas grinned. "We'll buy fruit, too," he said, tugging a long row of multicolored lollipops from a hanger. He placed them in the cart and Tony whimpered for one.

"Okay, big guy," Jonas said, and he proceeded to tear a lollipop from the row and hand it to Tony.

"But we haven't paid for that yet," Robin said.

"Look around," Jonas told her. "All the mothers are doing it. I'm sure the store manager won't mind if it's going to keep Tony quiet."

She looked around her dubiously, but, sure enough, many of the mothers had opened boxes of oat cereal, raisins, cookies or candy. Robin saw one young child with a graham cracker in one fist and a piece of banana in the other.

"Okay," Robin finally relented, but she saw that her nephew had already been sucking on a grape lollipop long enough for him to dribble purple saliva on the bib of his overalls.

As they traveled the aisles they discovered what each of them liked to eat. Jonas touted himself as an amateur gourmet chef.

"That's good," Robin remarked, "because I can barely boil water."

She told him that her job writing articles for a food magazine made it important for her to eat out. A lot.

"Doesn't that get old after a while?" he asked.

"It sure does. There are times when I wish I'd never see another restaurant."

"Well," Jonas said, "we'll fix you some good home cookin' while you're here." He cast her a sidelong glance. "You might even want to spend some time in the kitchen learning from the pro."

"Maybe," she muttered, but she seriously doubted it. The farther she stayed from Jonas, the better.

When they reached the produce aisle, Robin scanned the shelf of bananas for a bunch that was nice and ripe. Tony just might like to have some sliced up in his oatmeal tomorrow morning. She reached up high and picked six big yellow ones. When she turned to put them in the cart, she saw that Jonas had moved about ten feet from her.

She froze, her heart in her throat. Tony was standing up in the seat and Jonas was preoccupied with choosing oranges. The baby wobbled, righted himself and then reached out toward the perfectly shaped symmetrical hill of bright yellow lemons in front of him.

Dear God, please don't let him fall.

"Jonas!" she called, "the baby."

At least a dozen people turned to stare. Jonas's eyes widened in horror and he grabbed Tony's outstretched arm. Robin ran to help.

Jonas plunked Tony onto his butt in the seat, not noticing that the baby had come away with a fat lemon—from the bottom of the pile. Robin saw three pieces of fruit tumble to the floor where they rolled in crazy circles. She threw herself across the entire display. With her arms spread wide, she pressed her chest and stomach against the lemons, hoping to keep as many of them as possible from falling off the display.

With her cheek snug against one huge lemon, Robin moved her eyes and saw Jonas settling Tony into the seat of the cart.

"Jonas," she said, but with the lemon poking into her jaw it was impossible for her to speak loud enough to get his attention.

"Jonas," she tried again. This time he lifted his head and looked down at where she was sprawled across the display of lemons.

"Gee, Robin," he said. "You really shouldn't hoard all the citrus fruit for yourself."

Robin made to rise from her precarious position—she wanted so badly to knock a knot right on his head—but she felt quite a few of the lemons slide down the yellow tower so she remained with her body plastered against the fruit.

"I see a woman right over there," he quipped, "who looks like she wants to make a big pitcher of lemonade."

The sound of Jonas's chuckle grated in her ears.

If she ever got loose of this fruit, she'd kill him.

"Help me, you idiot."

"Oh, here comes someone," he whispered close to her ear. "She looks like she wants to bake a lemon meringue pie. You'd better give over a few lemons." He straightened up. "Come on, just a few."

"So help me, Jonas, when I get up from here, I'm going to—"

"Is there a problem here, folks?"

The young man who asked the question stood directly behind her, so she couldn't see him. But she was so relieved that help had arrived. It was obvious she wasn't going to get any from Jonas.

"Yes," Jonas told him boldly, "the problem is this lady. She won't let me have any lemons."

Robin heard the laughter then and realized that several people had gathered to watch the show. She felt her face flame red-hot and her underarms prickled with perspiration. Jonas was making a spectacle of her. And to think, she'd only dived on the display of fruit so he wouldn't have lemons bouncing all around his feet.

"Let me try to help you."

The young man's voice was like manna from heaven. He slipped his hand between her cheek and the fruit. She lifted her head while he steadied the loose lemons. As the man did the same thing to her arm, she realized that Jonas worked on getting her other arm free.

Before too many more embarrassing moments passed, Robin stood and gave a sigh of relief. The six or so customers who had stopped to watch applauded her release. Her head dipped as she tried to hide her disgrace.

But then she realized that several of them murmured, "Good job."

"Yeah," the man said. "Thanks for saving my display."

These people weren't making fun of her, she realized. They were praising her. She smiled at them. Then she glared at Jonas. He might have wanted to humiliate her, but he'd failed.

Out of the corner of her eye, she saw a flash of yellow. Her gaze darted to Tony just in time to see him raise a big lemon to his mouth and bite down.

Her lips puckered and her mouth watered just seeing the sour look on the child's face. Tony blinked several times and then handed the lemon over to her.

"Bad," he said. Then he wiped his tongue off with his fingers.

"Here," she said. "Lick on your lollipop."

She guided the grape flavored pop into his mouth and his smile returned,

"Take this," she ordered, plunking the mangled lemon into Jonas's palm. And without looking back, she started off toward the checkout counter.

Jonas turned to the produce worker, a question in his eyes.

"Sorry, sir," the man said. "You'll have to buy that."

Jonas stood in the doorway of Tony's bedroom and gazed at Robin rocking the baby. After Robin had told him exactly what she thought of him in the parking lot of the supermarket, things had gone downhill quickly. She refused to speak to him all the way home. They'd even put away the groceries in silence.

He hadn't meant to embarrass her by his joshing in the produce department. He'd thought his wisecracking would pull the attention from her and place it onto himself. But Robin had adamantly believed he'd been trying to make her a laughingstock.

When she refused to listen to reason, he had nudged her a little with one or two witty remarks. He probably shouldn't have, but he'd loved to see her dark eyes come alive with all that spit and vinegar. Surprisingly he'd found her anger very tantalizing.

Their argument would probably still be going on if it hadn't been for Tony turning cranky. Soon after they'd returned home from the store, the baby began to whine. He couldn't seem to get comfortable enough to take even a short nap in the afternoon. However, Tony did seem to get some relief when Robin rocked him—as long as Jonas remained nearby. Both Jonas and Robin had come to the conclusion that Tony found security in her hugs because her body was more like Sara's than Jonas's was. So, Robin had rocked him for over an hour, and he'd slept fitfully for only a few minutes.

When he awoke, Jonas and Robin had taken him to the park, hoping that the fresh air would revive his spirits. The trip had been a disaster.

They had returned home, tried, to no avail, to get Tony to eat some supper, and here they were, hours past the baby's bedtime, still rocking, still soothing him with gentle words.

As Jonas watched Robin cuddle Tony, he thought that one good thing had come of the baby's cranky spell— Robin looked too darned tired to be angry at him any longer. He thought it ironic that Tony cleaved to her so, when just this morning he wanted nothing whatsoever to do with her.

Robin looked up at him, weariness dulling her deep-set brown eyes.

"Do you think this is something other than *g-r-i-e-f*?" she asked, spelling out the word as though she were afraid Tony might understand and be more upset.

"Well, Amy did tell us that he cried himself to sleep every night." Jonas kept his voice as quiet as possible.

Robin sighed. "But this has been going on since this afternoon."

He nodded. "How about if I call Amy and ask her what she thinks?"

Laying her head back and closing her eyes, Robin said, "Sounds like a good idea to me."

Jonas left the room as quietly as possible, knowing that if Tony noticed his disappearance he'd become agitated. He grabbed the cordless phone and then Sara and Jeff's address book from the drawer in the kitchen. He was back upstairs in under a minute.

He looked up Amy's number and punched the keys on the telephone pad. It had rung at least a dozen times before he gave up.

"She's not home," he whispered to Robin.

"Call the pediatrician," she said.

"But it's after hours."

"Jonas, we could have a sick little boy on our hands here," she told him. "Do you know what signs to look for? Has he been acting normal today? Are you confident enough in your judgment to say he's *not* sick? Can it hurt to simply ask the doctor's opinion?"

"Okay, okay." Even as he said the words, he flipped through the book to find the doctor's number.

He gave the answering service all the information and was told that the doctor would call him within the hour.

Robin continued to rock Tony in the silent darkness of the room, and Jonas stood in the doorway watching helplessly.

Finally the baby dozed off with his head resting against Robin's breast. Jonas thought it was a lovely, peaceful image.

When the phone rang, Tony didn't stir. Jonas spoke to the doctor, took note of his instructions and cut the connection.

"The doctor wants us to take Tony's temperature," Jonas told her. "I'm going to find a thermometer."

He began his search in the bathroom off the hallway and happily discovered Sara's first aid kit. The covered plastic box contained swabs, gauze pads, antibiotic ointment, a thermometer, alcohol, and Jonas's eyes lit up when he saw a book on baby ailments and remedies.

"Hallelujah," he said to himself.

He returned to Tony's bedroom, his arms loaded with medical paraphernalia. Somehow, he didn't quite feel so helpless anymore.

"Here," he said, handing Robin the thermometer. "The doctor wants you to take Tony's temperature. You need to insert it—"

"Oh, no." She cut him off. "When I took this job, I never agreed to insert anything anywhere. That's the doctor's job. It's what he went to medical school for."

Jonas couldn't hold back his chuckle. "But, Robin, the doctor needs to know—"

"I am not going to wake up this child to do something to him that I know will make him very unhappy," she said. "So, if you're still determined to know if he's running a fever or not, then you're more than welcome to insert that thermometer—"

Again he chuckled. "Okay," he said. He picked up the baby book. "Let's just see if we can get the information some other way."

He quickly found instructions on "taking baby's temperature" and was pleased to see that "inserting" wasn't the only way to get the job done.

"It says here," Jonas told Robin, "that we can place the thermometer under his arm."

"I think I can handle that," she said.

As they waited for the recommended three minutes to elapse, Jonas looked up Tony's symptoms in the back of the book.

"He could have colic," he said. He read further. "Or he could be teething. It says here that molars sometimes cause a great deal of pain as the tooth breaks through the gum." After studying for a few more silent moments, Jonas closed the book and took the thermometer from Robin's fingers.

He nodded. "He's got a slight fever. But nothing to be worried about. Let me feel." He slipped his index finger between Tony's lips and probed the baby's gums. Tony stirred when Jonas touched a swollen spot in the back of his mouth.

"That's it," Jonas said. "He's cutting a molar. It feels really sore, too. Poor fella."

"He's out like a light, though," Robin observed in a tired voice.

Jonas nodded. "Let me put him in his crib."

He put the baby to bed and tucked a cotton blanket over his bare legs.

"We didn't check his diaper," Robin said.

"Let's worry about that later."

Jonas held out his hand to help her from the chair, and he was pleased when she took it without hesitation.

"Come on downstairs and I'll fix us both a cup of decaf," he offered.

Robin stretched her neck, then reached around to massage her sore muscles. "Sounds good to me," she said.

They went downstairs, Robin to the family room to prop up her feet, and Jonas to the kitchen to prepare the coffee.

He poured the steaming hot liquid into mugs, thinking how great Robin had been with Tony. She'd stayed calm even though he knew she was feeling frustrated with the baby's tears. Maybe she did have a maternal bone or two in her body. One that he and his sister, Sara, had missed seeing.

When he came into the family room, he stopped in the doorway and smiled. Robin lay on the couch, her eyes closed, her lashes dark, thick fans against creamy cheeks. Her deep, even breathing told him she was sound asleep.

He placed her mug on the table and sat down in the easy chair to drink his coffee. But something told him he was going to enjoy the view much more than the refreshment.

Chapter Five

Something had changed. Robin couldn't quite put her finger on what it was, but her relationship with Jonas was...different. They'd been living together in her brother's house now for more than a week. And their working routine was running very smoothly.

Jonas had been right about the time span needed for her to gain Tony's trust. After just three days, the baby clamored for her attention just as often as he called for Jonas's. She continued to feel overwhelmed with heart-wrenching love every time her nephew called, "Bob-in! Bob-in!" and demanded that she follow him as he examined some new and wondrous discovery.

The three of them had made some amazing strides over the days they'd lived together. After the teething incident during which Tony was miserable for nearly two full days as his first molar pushed its way through his swollen gum, Robin and Jonas decided to visit the baby's pediatrician. The man told them many things about Tony that they hadn't known: he had no food allergies to date, he was prone to ear infections, he hadn't contracted chicken pox yet and probably wouldn't until he began nursery school. The information made both her and Jonas feel more confident in their job as Tony's guardian.

But Robin felt they still had so much further to go. Yes, Tony was comfortable with her now; he even enjoyed their mornings together. But he would constantly go searching for Jonas where he worked in the office. Tony would only stay in the room with his uncle for the briefest of moments, but every hour or so—just like clockwork—he'd toddle to the office and reassure himself that Jonas was still around.

Robin smiled, thinking about the manner in which Jonas greeted Tony each time the child interrupted his work. He always smiled brightly and called out a hearty "hello," as though it were the first time he'd seen the baby that day and that he was terribly grateful for the visit. Jonas never showed any signs of irritation or frustration over Tony's intrusion.

The funny thing was that the baby did the same thing to her when it was Jonas's turn to watch him in the afternoon and she was busy writing her article on Hawaiian food.

She and Jonas had talked about his behavior late one evening after the nightmare of putting him to bed was over and they had decided that having his parents whisked away from him had demolished any sense of security he had. They agreed that if Tony wanted to check on them a thousand times each day, it would be okay.

She sighed heavily as she thought about putting Tony to bed each evening. It truly was a nightmare. So much so that Robin hated to see the sun setting on the horizon. But then again, afternoon nap time was horrible, too. It was during these times that the baby grieved so for his parents that he simply couldn't be consoled.

Dealing with their nephew's problems had somehow changed Robin and Jonas's relationship. They had begun to focus more on Tony, which was as it should be, and less on nitpicking with each other.

Because priority was placed on making Tony happy and content, it seemed that Jonas's sarcastic witticisms grew fewer and fewer, and because of that, Robin's criticism of him lessened also. All in all, arguments between Robin and Jonas had become a thing of the past. It certainly was nice to wake up in the morning and know that the day with Jonas would be pleasant and calm rather than fraught with arguments and strife.

But there was bad that went along with this good. Since Jonas was keeping his taunting observations to a bare minimum, Robin was left unarmed against the attraction she felt for the man. It used to be that he would snuff out any desire she felt for him simply by opening his mouth. But because he was being very careful to keep the household atmosphere as tension free as possible, he was making it a point to be polite and amiable. And it was killing her!

Yes, Jonas was succeeding in lessening the angry tension between them, but his gentlemanly behavior was only heightening a different kind of tension—sexual tension.

She could actually feel the heavy pulse in the air when they were together. And she was beginning to wonder if he was feeling it, too. She hoped not. If he did, she'd feel—

"So, did he finally go to sleep?"

Although Jonas's voice was feather soft, it startled her from her reverie. He smiled when she lifted her gaze to his. The gentle concern displayed on his features made her heart pound. She wished he wouldn't be so...so...nice to her. It only complicated her feelings.

She nodded, and then in an effort to avoid his eyes, she glanced around the family room. "I really should pick up some of these toys," she murmured, "before someone falls and breaks their neck."

His hand on her shoulder was warm and firm. "Don't you move," he told her, easing himself down on the couch beside her. "I know you've had a rough morning dealing with Tony. You deserve to just sit here and relax for a few minutes."

His fingers gently massaged her taut shoulder muscle while his soothing tone did the same to her soul.

Hot tears sprang to her eyes, splintering the bright afternoon sunlight that filtered in through the white gauzy curtains. What was wrong with her? she wondered. Tony *had* been extraordinarily rambunctious this morning, but Robin couldn't help having a sneaking suspicion that this unexpected lachrymal feeling had more to do with Jonas's kindness and caring toward her. But she didn't dare let on that his interest affected her in this way. Heck, if he knew he was causing her to cry, he would have a field day!

She rested her head against the back of the couch and closed her eyes.

"Jonas," she whispered hoarsely, "we have to do something for Tony. He misses his mommy and daddy."

"I know he does," Jonas said.

His warm fingers now trailed a silky path up and down her upper arm. She knew he was only trying to console her, but she wished he'd go sit across the room. That would certainly make her life a lot easier.

"But," he continued softly, "unfortunately there's absolutely nothing we can do to ease his grief. We can be here for him. We can love him and hug him. Feed him and play with him. But we're not his mom and dad. And we can't bring them back. No matter how much we might want to."

"It's just that it breaks my heart to see him cry, to hear him call out for them over and over." The silent tear that slipped down her cheek had nothing to do with Jonas. It was for the frightened, lonely little boy who slept fitfully upstairs in the crib.

His palm cupped her elbow now, his thumb rubbing a slow rhythm over her tender skin.

He sighed heavily. "I have been thinking," he said.

She lifted her head and stared at him. At this point, she'd do anything to save Tony some of the anguish he was having to suffer.

"Where is it written that Tony has to have a set bedtime?" he asked.

"What do you mean?"

He shrugged. "Well, why do we have to put him to bed at precisely eight-thirty every night?"

She felt her forehead wrinkle with a frown of confusion. "Because that's his bedtime," she answered simply. "He's tired out by then. Besides, you were the one who said that Sara kept him on a strict routine. Bath time, snack time, bedtime."

He removed his fingers from her arm to rake them through his hair. The spot on her arm where he'd been touching her felt cold and empty.

"But Sara's gone," he stated, the first signs of frustration showing in his voice. "And we're here. And we need to... try something different."

After a moment of silence, Robin said, "Okay, so you don't want an eight-thirty bedtime." She looked at him, waiting for him to explain his idea further.

"Well," he said, "let's give him his bath—"

"It's your turn tonight, by the way." She couldn't help the grin that crept over her lips. Tony loved to splash, so bath time was a very wet and wild undertaking.

"Yeah, I know."

He, too, smiled and Robin felt her heart leap. Why did he have to be so good-looking?

"Anyway," he continued, "let's give him a bath, feed him his snack and then all three of us curl up on the sofa here together and watch cartoon videos." He pointed at the oak cabinet by the television. "There's certainly enough of them to choose from over there."

She nodded slowly as the idea took shape in her head. At this point, she'd try anything.

"Hopefully Tony will fall asleep right here and I can carry him upstairs to his crib." Jonas shrugged. "It's worth a try, don't you think?"

"Yes," she said quietly, realizing there was a quality in her voice that conveyed every ounce of frustration she was feeling. "Yes, I do."

Although she was no longer looking him in the face, she could feel his eyes on her. The silence grew thick and heavy, and Robin felt something stirring in the air— something that had nothing whatsoever to do with Tony and his problem.

Jonas draped his arm along the back of the couch, his hand coming to rest on her shoulder. The heat of his touch seemed scorchingly hot, and Robin had to force herself not to flinch.

It wasn't that the pressure of his fingers on her was uncomfortable, not by any means. But the feel of his touch conjured confusing emotions in her, feelings and urges she either couldn't identify or didn't want to deal with. He made her feel out of control. He made her feel as though she wanted his touch on more of her than just her shoulders. The curve of her neck seemed to call out for his attentive fingers. Her cheeks and lips wanted to feel his warmth. Deep inside her, curling tendrils of heat spiraled and writhed in wild abandon.

"Robin?"

Her eyelids flew open and she blinked several times. She hadn't even realized she had closed her eyes, hadn't been aware of just how focused she'd become on the touch of his fingers on her shoulder.

She watched his mouth curl into a tiny grin. *Get ready,* she told herself. *He's about to say something mean and humiliating.*

"I thought maybe you'd fallen asleep," he said gently. "You were breathing so deeply and evenly."

Not sleeping, she silently admitted. Simply concentrating on something she had no business concentrating on.

"You've worked so hard with Tony all week," he said. "Why don't you take this afternoon off?"

Wait a minute, her subconscious warned. Nothing he'd said had been mean or nasty. He hadn't embarrassed her or humiliated her. She felt her eyes narrow with suspicion. What was he up to?

"When Tony wakes up we can go to the mall or something," he continued softly. "Or if you'd rather be alone, you could go do some shopping by yourself." His smile widened. "Just think, a whole afternoon without work or men cluttering up your life."

It sounded like heaven. Wasting the entire afternoon away strolling through the mall, window-shopping with Jonas and Tony. They would laugh at Tony's antics. They would enjoy seeing the world through the baby's eyes. They'd have fun. Together. It sounded terrifying.

"No," she stated emphatically, straightening her spine so she no longer reclined against the couch, so Jonas's hand no longer rested on her shoulder.

She felt stronger now that she didn't have to contend with the soft pressure of his warm fingers in her skin.

"No," she repeated. "I have to work. My editors are expecting my article by the end of the week."

It was a bald-faced lie. Her editors had told her to take her time recovering from the loss of her family, take her time getting used to dealing with her nephew. But her editors knew nothing about the problems she was having dealing with her feelings regarding Jonas.

Jonas seemed to withdraw. He crossed his arms over his chest. His green eyes closed off all emotion. There was a coolness about him that made Robin feel suddenly alienated and alone.

Good, she thought. This she could deal with. This wall of detachment would enable her to focus on learning all she could about rearing a child, so that in eight months' time she could break the news to Jonas that *she* was the one who would raise the baby.

"You're sure?" His question was curt.

"Yes," she told him. "Quite sure."

She rose and went to the doorway where she paused.

"But I will join you and Tony tonight," she said. "Your idea sounds like a good one. And I really hope it works."

The coldness in his green gaze softened and he nodded.

As Robin turned and walked away, she was left wondering why she'd been impelled to compliment him. She felt that her praise only served to soften the mortar between the bricks holding together the wall of detachment she had so hastily built, and she couldn't fathom why she'd do such a thing.

* * *

Her arms were elbow-deep in sudsy dishwater. Her stomach began to churn anxiously during dinner. Tony's nap had been cut short when a neighbor's dog barked furiously at a squirrel this afternoon, so the baby was tired even though his usual bedtime was over an hour away.

Tony had been peevish and contrary at the dinner table. He'd fussed and picked at his food, taking great pleasure in squishing his green beans between his fingers. Robin and Jonas had looked at each other, both obviously hesitant to discipline their nephew yet not wanting to encourage such behavior, either.

Finally Jonas had simply taken Tony upstairs for his bath.

So, Robin was cleaning up the mess left from dinner.

She twisted all the water from the dishcloth and went to wipe up the bits of beans from the tray of Tony's high chair. When she finished with that chore, she emptied the soapy water from the sink and then swept the floor.

Her chest felt heavy with apprehension. What would they do if Jonas's plan didn't work? Would she have to endure another night of listening to Tony's heartrending sobs? She didn't think her nerves could take it.

She remembered the agony in Jonas's face as he, too, tried to comfort Tony. She didn't think he could take it, either.

Hopefully Jonas's idea of having Tony fall asleep in front of the television would work and neither of them would have to experience another night of anguish.

Robin bent to sweep the dirt onto the dustpan.

"Here we are," Jonas announced.

She turned and had to smile.

Tony was shiny clean, his curly hair plastered to his head in wet ringlets. But what made her smile was the fact that

Jonas looked just as shiny clean. His hair, too, was slicked back, and she noticed that he had on a different shirt than what he'd been wearing when he'd taken the baby upstairs.

"Did you decide to have a bath, too?" she asked.

"I didn't decide." He pointed at Tony. "He did. He had me so wet, I might as well have climbed into the tub with him."

Tony evidently realized what they were talking about because he giggled and shouted, "Splash!"

Jonas shook his head and Robin couldn't hold back her chuckle.

His gaze became serious. "You're just finishing up? Tony really did a job on the kitchen, didn't he?"

"It wasn't too bad," she told him. "Besides, I'd rather give the kitchen a bath any day than—" she tickled Tony's rib " —give this kid a bath."

The toddler squirmed in Jonas's arms and laughed.

"Okay," Jonas said, "what are we going to snack on tonight?"

Robin knew concern was showing in her eyes when she looked at Jonas. "Do you think he ate enough dinner?" she asked. "Should we be giving him goodies when he didn't finish—"

"It's all right," he said. "This one time won't hurt." Then he shrugged. "He was too tired to eat his veggies. Maybe he'll be too tired to eat some ice cream."

"Yea, yea, yea." Tony chanted the tiny word, propelling himself up and down in Jonas's embrace.

Jonas's green eyes sparkled, obviously realizing what kind of response the mention of ice cream would elicit from his nephew.

Robin scooped up three bowls of vanilla ice cream and carried them into the family room. She placed them on the coffee table and sat down on the couch. Then she glanced over to where Jonas was inspecting the buttons on the videocassette recorder while Tony slid black plastic cassettes from their cardboard casings.

"Do you have any idea how this works?" Jonas asked her. "I mean, have you had a chance to use it while we've been here?"

He wasn't looking at her, so he didn't see her shake her head. "Sorry," she said.

"Well, I may be a mechanical misfit," he said, "however, I know there's got to be an On button and a Play button." He scratched his head. "But I can't find either one."

Jonas sat back on his heels just about the time Tony toddled over with a cassette in both hands. He popped the tape into the slot with only the tiniest of trouble, then he pushed the button that turned on the television.

The tape slid smoothly into the machine, rewound itself and immediately began to play.

Jonas's shoulders shook as he laughed. He looked back at Robin. "Couldn't be easier than that, now could it?"

She expected to see colorful cartoon characters and hear the lively music associated with such comic capers, and when she didn't, the serious implications didn't strike her right away.

The scene on the television screen was blurry white—it was snow, Robin realized. Deep snow.

A woman and child came into view.

"Wave at Daddy."

An icy chill ran down Robin's spine as she recognized Sara's voice. A younger Tony waved and grinned at the camera.

"Hey, Tony."

Robin couldn't see her brother on-screen, but simply hearing him speak was enough to bring tears to her eyes. Pressing her fingertips to her lips, she stood and watched in paralyzed silence. She hazily noticed that Jonas and Tony also seemed hypnotized by the unexpected image on the television. None of them spoke. None of them moved. None of them even breathed.

The camera was jostled as it was placed on a table or some other smooth surface. Then Jeff and Sara were both in the picture, showing their son how to make a snowball. The baby on-screen frowned at the white powder, touched it and drew back his hand.

"Look, baby," Sara said to her son. "It's snow."

"Mama."

Robin's gaze flew to Tony when she heard him whisper his mother's name, and there was no other way to describe his tone except to say it was in ecstasy.

"Jonas?" Robin's voice was sharp with anxiety. She hadn't realized she'd begun to cry. Her tears flowed freely, and the sorrow and indecision she felt were more than she could handle. She desperately needed for Jonas to take control of the situation.

But when he looked at her, she saw his eyes were red and moist, and the grief he was feeling was as plain as if it were spelled out in block letters across his forehead.

Dear Lord, what should she do?

With the speed of lightning, Tony dived at the television as though he meant to go straight through the thick screen.

"Mama!" he cried, and at the same instant, he smacked his head against the glass.

Robin gasped as the laws of physics threw the baby backward with enough momentum to plop him onto his diapered butt. Jonas had evidently gained some of his senses back, at least enough to snatch Tony's arm and keep him from cracking his head on the floor.

Tony's scream was filled with pain and shock and the frustration of finally finding his long lost parents only to discover he couldn't get to them.

"Off!" Robin yelled. "Turn off the television!"

Jonas looked at her for the briefest second before he swiveled around and snapped off the TV.

Robin rounded the coffee table and bent down on her knees beside Tony. He cried piteously, an angry, red lump swelling on his head.

"I had no idea," Jonas said, his voice filled with self-loathing. "I should have checked the movie he had in his hand. I never thought about family videos."

Between the baby's wet, hiccuping sobs, he called out for his mother and father, pointing and straining toward the blank television screen.

"I... I had no idea," Jonas repeated, the words barely heard above Tony's wails.

"Jonas—" she placed her hand firmly on his shoulder to get his attention "—go into the kitchen and put some ice in a dish towel."

When he looked at her his green eyes looked dazed.

Robin raised her tone. "We need to get some ice on Tony's forehead."

Jonas nodded and rose to his feet. When he was gone, Robin picked up Tony and cradled him against her shoulder. She rocked him back and forth until the small of her back began to throb.

With wrapped ice in hand, Jonas returned.

"Let's take him upstairs," she suggested. "I'm sure he's going to cry himself to sleep again tonight."

Jonas glanced at the television, obviously realizing how miserably his idea had failed. He nodded.

"It's going to be okay," she felt impelled to say. Robin had no idea if everything would be okay, however she couldn't help but offer the poor man some kind of comfort, even though it was small. She would have reached out to him, but Tony was a big baby and she needed both hands to hold on to him.

Once they were upstairs in Tony's room, the situation seemed to grow worse. The baby squirmed and cried when Jonas placed the cold pack against his head. He buried his face in Robin's shoulder, and when she insisted that he let her put the ice on his bump, Tony called out for Jonas and the ritual repeated itself.

"What are we doing to the kid?" Jonas finally asked as he passed Tony to Robin for the third time. "We're making him miserable."

And ourselves, Robin silently agreed, gently patting Tony's back.

"Tony," Jonas said, his voice filled with a false brightness that would only fool a nitwit, "want to play with some toys? Uncle Jonas will build you a tower of blocks."

The baby never even lifted his head from Robin's shoulder. She raised her hand into an awkward position, trying to maneuver the cold towel to Tony's head.

"Forget that," Jonas told her. "We need to get his mind off of *them.*" He said the pronoun in a mere whisper. "Tony, come play with me." He went to the toy box and sat cross-legged in front of it.

The baby pushed himself away from Robin and she put him down on the floor. But rather than going to his uncle, Tony turned and strode right out the door of his bedroom.

"Where's he going?" Robin asked Jonas.

Jonas shrugged, then pushed himself to a stand. Then he and Robin went out the door.

The hallway was empty and Robin questioned Jonas with her eyes. Jonas shook his head.

"Tony?" he called. "Where are you, son?"

"Mama."

Tony's voice was hoarse from crying, and Robin frowned when she realized that he had pushed open the door of the master bedroom and had gone inside. The faint smell of Sara's perfume wafted around her. Robin fumbled for a moment before flipping on the light switch.

Her throat swelled tight with emotion and she actually pressed her hands against her chest, hoping her pained heart wouldn't tear right in two. Tears prickled her eyes as she looked at Tony standing on the floor at the head of his parents' bed, his tearstained face pressed against his mother's pillow.

Chapter Six

Twenty minutes later Robin came down the stairs slowly, weariness making every step heavy. She was tired, she knew, not just from soothing and consoling Tony, but also from the turmoil her emotions had endured through the pitiful and agonizing ordeal.

When they had found Tony leaning against his mother's pillow, she and Jonas had simply pulled the baby up onto the bed, and the three of them had lain there until Tony had finally cried himself to sleep. Robin had spent the time smoothing her hand over her nephew's silky curls. Jonas had patted and rubbed the baby's back.

After Tony had fallen to an exhausted sleep, Jonas had gently picked him up and took him to his crib with Robin close on his heels. Jonas had disappeared then, but she'd barely realized it because she'd been so focused on tucking Tony in for the night, making certain his favorite stuffed animal was nearby in case he awoke in the wee hours.

She'd stayed by his side for a while, trying to bolster herself, make herself believe that the baby would get over his parents' death, that everything would work out. Eventually. But the emotional episode had taken so much out of her, she was left feeling completely empty inside.

Her hand rested on the banister as she came down the last step. With rounded shoulders she turned down the hallway and made her way to the family room where she knew the bowls of ice cream she'd left there would be waiting, all melted and gone to waste, to be taken into the kitchen and dumped down the food disposal.

She came through the doorway and saw Jonas on his knees in front of the oak cabinet where the videos were stored. He was pulling them from the shelf and checking the titles. She noticed that there was a small stack of empty cardboard video cases on one side of him, a stack of movies on the other.

"They're all mixed up," he said, irritation evident in his voice. "These movies aren't in the proper cases. How is a person to know which movie he's about to choose if they aren't where they're supposed to be?"

The bowls of ice cream completely left her mind as she made a beeline toward Jonas. Even though her exhaustion made her feel sluggish and slow, she knew from the sound of his voice that Jonas needed her. Urgently.

"Jonas," she said softly, gently. "Stop."

She knelt down beside him and reached out to touch him on the shoulder.

"Jonas, it wasn't your fault," she said. "You had no way of knowing that the video would be a family movie."

He didn't stop his frantic task. "I *should* have known. I should have at least thought of the possibility that something like this could happen. I'm supposed to be the boy's guardian, damn it." His tone was filled with self-reproach. "I'm supposed to protect him from harm."

Robin swallowed the lump of emotion that rose painfully in her throat. She understood exactly how Jonas was feeling. She, too, felt a tremendous responsibility for what had happened. She, too, felt that she should have realized there might be family movies mixed up with the videos. But she hadn't.

He jerked another movie from its cardboard casing, slapped the box down on one side of him, the video on the other.

"I'm supposed to protect him, too." Her voice had gone all whispery with emotion.

Lost in his own self-blame, Jonas said, "What I should do is just get rid of all these family movies. Then I'll know for certain this won't ever happen again."

Robin's hand fell to her side and she leaned her weight back on her heels. "Why didn't we think of that before?" she asked him.

He looked at her for the first time since she'd come into the room.

"Because, Robin," he said, his tone edged with frustration, "we've never had an occasion to use the VCR."

"I'm not talking about just the family movies." She reached up and tucked a curling tendril of her hair behind her ear. "I'm talking about pictures, too—vacation snapshots, family portraits, that kind of thing."

Robin could see she had his undivided attention now.

"There are pictures all over this house," she said. "It's no wonder that Tony can't get his mom and dad out of his mind. Their images are hanging on every wall of this house."

It was true. And almost as if the far wall had magnetic powers that attracted their eyes, they both turned and stared at the arrangement of family photos.

"They *are* everywhere," Jonas whispered.

"And every time Tony sees them—"

"He's reminded of Jeff and Sara," he concluded.

Robin nodded.

There was an intensity in Jonas's green gaze when he looked at her. "Let's pack them away," he said. "The pictures, the movies, and anything else that might remind Tony of Sara and Jeff."

For a moment, she said nothing. The doubt that flared inside her was like a scalding poker that made her reach out and grasp Jonas's forearm with both hands.

"Wait," she said. "Are you sure this is the right thing for us to do?" She swallowed, feeling strong emotions churning, churning, threatening to surface. "I mean, would Jeff and Sara want us to take down all their family pictures? Would they want us to take them away from Tony?"

Sudden anger glittered in Jonas's eyes. It seemed to come from nowhere and it startled Robin.

"Look," he snapped, "are we going to sit around second-guessing ourselves, or are we going to do what we think is right for that little boy upstairs?"

"Jonas—" her hands slid down his arm until she was cradling his fingers in hers "—I'm not finding fault, here. I'm not placing blame. It was my idea, remember?"

He sighed slowly, his anger receding.

"I simply want to make sure we're doing the right thing," she said.

After clearing his throat, he said, "I'm sorry. It's just that..."

Robin shook her head. "Don't apologize. I'm sharing every bit of your frustration. We *do* need to help Tony get through this. We need to do whatever it takes to make his life a little less miserable."

"Okay then," he said. "I'll finish here and you start pulling down pictures."

Even though she felt she and Jonas were doing the right thing, she couldn't deny the heavy blanket of sadness that enveloped her as she gently took picture after picture down from the walls of the house. There were so many of them.

She traveled from room to room, scanning the walls and furniture. She found framed photos everywhere, she even came upon an unframed picture of Jeff and Sara kissing that had been pinned up on the inside door of the medicine cabinet in the master bathroom. Her hand hesitated, thinking it unlikely that Tony would ever venture into this room. But finally she pulled the picture from its resting place, feeling that if she was going to do the job, she might as well do a thorough one.

Once her arms were full, she'd make a trip to the family room and deposit the pictures on the coffee table. After her third trip back to the family room, she saw that Jonas had come up with a box from somewhere and was wrapping the picture frames in newspaper before carefully, gently placing them into the box.

He glanced up at her, a small, sad smile on his lips. He dipped his head to continue his job, and Robin was completely overtaken by a wretched depression. She looked down at the stacks of pictures, movies and family albums that were scattered across the tabletop.

She never realized it until now, but these pictures were all she had left of her brother. There were no recent memories floating around in her head to remember him by. The black depths of the emptiness inside her yawned wide.

Why, oh, why had she waited so long before understanding what he meant to her? Why had it taken his death to make her realize that she should have been running *toward* her family, not away from them?

Feeling her bottom lip begin to tremble uncontrollably, she scurried out the doorway and into the kitchen. She leaned against the counter, her fingertips pressed tightly against her mouth.

As Robin stood there, she understood for the first time in her life that she was all alone. Her father, her mother and now her brother were lost to her forever. The sorrow that welled within her was too great to keep inside. She closed her eyes against the tears, but they came anyway. They coursed down her cheeks, and before Robin realized it, her shoulders were shaking, her throat swelled and ached as the sobs racked her body.

The sound of Robin crying had Jonas on his feet and in the kitchen in an instant. He understood the sorrow she was feeling; he felt it himself. Without saying a word, he wrapped his arms around her and held on.

He could feel the grief pour from her—in the way she clutched his back and hugged him to her tightly, in the heat of her teardrops as they soaked the fabric of his shirt at the shoulder.

She needed to cry, he knew that. She needed to mourn. Hell, so did he. The both of them had been so involved in helping Tony, in easing his pain, neither one of them had given themselves the opportunity to grieve for the loved ones that they had lost.

He and Robin had suffered, too. But both of them had been too stubborn, too stiff-necked to give in to it. And they were paying for it now.

Jonas hadn't shushed her, she realized. He hadn't said a bunch of empty, meaningless words in some attempt to console her. He'd simply held her, somehow knowing that that was what she needed, and she was so grateful for that.

Through the haze of her agony, Robin felt Jonas's breathing become ragged. She dragged her head from his shoulder and looked into his handsome face. The moisture that filled his eyes turned them to glittering emeralds. One tear spilled over and trailed down his cheek. Without thinking, she reached up and captured it on her fingertip, then pressed her palm against his jaw.

"I'm sorry," she whispered hoarsely. "I never meant to—"

He stopped her by placing his fingers gently against her lips. "Don't you dare apologize," he said.

His voice brushed against her skin like warm honey, sweet and liquescent. "Just know that I'm here for you."

What he said was simple, but it started fresh tears flowing. She'd never had that. She'd never had someone there for her. However, she knew deep down in her soul that it was nobody's fault but her own.

She slid her palm over the back of his hand and cradled her cheek against the warmth of his skin. Closing her eyes, she reveled in how alive he felt.

At that moment, she wanted to tell him everything she was feeling. She'd never confided in anyone in her life, but right now she felt an overwhelming need to make someone understand her.

With her tears flowing freely, she began, "Seeing Jeff there on the television...I was stunned. I felt...paralyzed.

I wanted so badly to reach out and hug him to me, to tell him how much I've missed him, how much I love him."

Jonas nodded. "I know," he said. "I felt the same way seeing Sara."

Robin squeezed her eyes shut. "But it's been over a year since I'd seen them." The words were painfully forced from her throat. "Why didn't I come and visit them more often? Why did I wait to know my brother until it was too late?"

Jonas remained silent, realizing that what was happening here to this woman was something more complicated than grieving for the loss of her brother. But he couldn't stop the frown that creased his forehead. What did she mean when she'd said she'd waited too long to get to know Jeff? How could she have a brother and not know him?

She nestled her face in the curve of his neck. Suddenly the questions that ran through his mind were forgotten as he became cognizant of his body's reaction to being pressed so tightly against Robin. The smell of spring flowers and warm sunshine wafted around him, and he fought the impulse to bury his nose in her curly hair.

Swallowing with difficulty, he silently railed at himself. *Control yourself, man. The woman needs sympathy and solace. Keep your desires out of this.*

He battled with his body.

Robin didn't know what had spurred her to do it. She didn't even realize she was thinking of doing it until after it was done. It could have been the feel of his arousal pressed against her hip. It could have been the warm and woodsy smell of him. It could have been the way his big, strong hands gently massaged her back. Whatever it was, it put a thought into her head—she wanted to stop the questions that spun in her brain, she wanted to stop the guilt and the sadness and the pain, and she wanted to *feel*. She wanted to feel alive.

She only had to turn her head a fraction and her lips were pressing against the hot skin of his neck. She raised her mouth a little higher, loving the roughness of his whiskers against her sensitive lips.

Inhaling his scent deeply into her lungs, she rose up on her tiptoes, closed her eyes and took his earlobe between her teeth. She suckled it gently before kissing her way down his jaw. She felt and heard his reaction, and her heart leapt with joy.

She was alive! She could feel!

Stopping at his chin long enough to nip the skin, she soothed the spot with her tongue and then moved up his jaw to his other ear.

Robin relished his reaction to her kisses. His heart pounded beneath her palms, his blood pulsed hot. She could see it, she could feel it. And it was wonderful.

"Robin."

Her mouth was pressed against his throat when he said her name and the vibration did something to her. The passion that had been slowly building inside her now accelerated with alarming speed.

She gasped when he pulled her from him. There was a silent question in his gaze as he stared down at her.

"Please, Jonas," she said, not caring that her voice sounded like that of someone starved and in desperate need of sustenance. "Help me."

He searched her eyes. But then he buried his fingers in her hair and covered her mouth with his.

His kiss was sweet, and hot. And she lost herself in the feel of it. His tongue played lightly on her lips, patiently waiting for an invitation to enter. She gave him more than just an invitation, she parted her lips and met him with a passionate heat that startled even herself.

He groaned, and her body reacted to the deep, rich sound of it—her breasts grew full and heavy, her stomach jumped with giddy anticipation, her skin seemed to call out for his touch. A hot, wild urgency flickered to life inside her—an urgency that was both frightening and exhilarating at the same time.

She wanted to get closer to him, though pressed against him as she was, she thought it impossible. But Jonas proved her wrong.

As he kissed her, he lifted her so that she sat on the edge of the counter. Her knees spread and he pressed his waist against the heat at the very core of her being. She sighed, and as if it was the most natural thing in the world to do, she wrapped her legs around his middle, pressing him even closer.

The taste of him, the feel of him, the smell of him—all these things made her feel more vibrant and full of life than she had in...in...Than in her whole entire life.

Slowly she weaved her fingers through his dark, silky hair and she realized just how badly she'd been wanting to feel its soft texture.

She felt his heart pounding. Or was that thumping from her heart? It must be hers, because the blood coursed through her veins at a rate that made her feel light-headed and wonderfully dizzy.

Sliding her hand down his back, she smiled against his mouth—his heart, too, was hammering a furious rhythm.

"What?" he whispered, his voice ragged.

She pushed her hair out of her face and smiled into his eyes. "Let's go upstairs."

He didn't hesitate. He pulled her off the counter, locked his hands around her waist and turned toward the hallway.

Squeezing her thighs against his middle, she held on for dear life. She kissed the tip of his nose, his temple, his lips, his chin.

His strong hands firmly cupped her rear as he climbed the stairs. She felt safe in his arms, and the security he lent only seemed to heighten her passion.

He pushed open the door of his room with his foot and Robin was relieved that he didn't take the few extra seconds it would have taken to get farther along the hallway to her room. She couldn't wait to feel his bare skin against hers.

With him supporting her, she loosened her grasp around his middle and set her feet onto the rug. The floor seemed to dip and sway as she unbuttoned his shirt with quick and nimble fingers. She slid the fabric from his shoulders and let it fall, and she inhaled deeply the warm male scent of his smooth skin.

Her hands played lightly over the muscular curves of his shoulders and chest. His dark, springy hair tickled her palms, and she circled the hard nubs of his nipples with her thumbs. His breath caught and held, and she chuckled deep in the back of her throat.

"You minx," he said, the words rusty with desire.

Looking directly into his eyes, she reached down and released the button of his pants and ever so slowly tugged down his zipper. Although she didn't linger there, she knew his arousal strained against the material of his trousers. Purposefully steering her touch away from that part of his body, she slid her fingers around the waistband of his pants.

His eyes dulled with need, and this time her low laughter was seductive, knowing.

"You're enjoying my discomfort, are you?" he whispered.

She was helpless against the grin that tugged and then lingered at one corner of her mouth.

"Actually," she finally said, "I'm enjoying it very much."

One of his dark brows rose. "Then I think it's my turn for a little enjoyment."

Before she realized what he intended to do, she felt the warm smoothness of his palms slip under her T-shirt. His hands grazed the sides of her breasts, releasing inside her a heady, tinkling sensation. He gently tugged the shirt over her head and tossed it aside.

His eyes were no longer on her face, and her breathing quickened as she realized that *she* was the cause of that rapt look in his green gaze.

Leisurely he dipped his index finger underneath the lacy edging of her bra, and as he moved up, up, up in a tortoiselike pace, the smoothness of his nail sliding flat against her tender flesh nearly brought tears of joy to her eyes. He continued the motion until the strap of her bra was curled in his finger. With a gentle tug, he pulled it over her shoulder, then bent and kissed the spot where the strap had been.

The moment his lips touched her skin, she felt her nipples tighten into taut buds beneath the satin of her bra.

He saw. He knew. And when he gazed into her face there was a teasing glint of sweet success in his eyes.

"Now this," he said. "This is good."

He leaned toward her to kiss the delicate curve of her neck, and she closed her eyes and tilted her head to give him full access.

It was then that it happened. The shadows of doubt crept into her mind: What on earth was she doing?

Along with the doubt came the sorrow and grief, anguish and pain that had closed in on her downstairs in the kitchen. When she reached up to touch Jonas's shoulder, she saw that her hand was trembling.

No! her mind screamed. She wanted to flee from those horrible feelings. She wanted to run away from her discovery of being all alone in the world. She didn't want to think about her brother's death, or her sister-in-law's death, or that Tony grieved so badly he couldn't fall asleep at night.

Jonas was alive. He was living, breathing. And his kisses, his touch made her feel energetic and vivacious. She wanted to lose herself in him. In this.

Taking him by the hand, she went to the bed and lay down, pulling him on top of her. His weight felt good. It felt right.

"Kiss me, Jonas," she said, not even minding the complete and utter desperation she heard in her voice.

He did kiss her, crushing his mouth to hers.

And Robin gratefully let herself be swept away.

It was after midnight. Bright moonlight filtered through the window, painting strokes of soft radiance across the shadows of his bedroom.

Jonas smoothed his palm over the creamy skin of Robin's shoulder. He couldn't believe what had happened between them. Couldn't believe that the woman beside him—the woman who, just a couple of weeks ago, he would have described as distant and cool—that very same woman had nearly scorched him with her passion.

He'd been blown away by the depth of her desire. The intensity of their lovemaking had been . . . mind-boggling . . . as nothing he'd ever experienced.

When he'd heard her crying in the kitchen, he had known she was grieving for her brother and he'd gone to her with the sole purpose of consoling her. He hadn't for a second thought that the compassion he'd meant to give would turn into an awesome, wondrous, totally unexpected sexual encounter.

But she had needed him, and he had realized that from the way she'd clung to him, from the things she'd said.

However, lying here with her in his arms, feeling the warmth of her body next to his, he couldn't help but wonder if he'd taken advantage of her need. She'd been weak in her grief. Had he pushed her to do something she normally wouldn't have done?

Guilt burned its way through his veins as if it were hot acid.

Should he apologize for what they did?

Hell, no, he decided. Apologizing would give her the impression that he regretted the experience. And he certainly didn't regret one thing about their time together. Not one kiss, one touch, one . . . anything.

No, he certainly had no intention of telling her he was sorry. If anything, he felt a tremendous urge to thank her for an extraordinary experience he'd never forget.

Robin sighed and he felt her breath brush across his chest like warm satin. The inside curve of her small foot rested against his shin. Tendrils of her curly hair were so close to his nose that all he had to do to smell the flowery fragrance of her was to inhale. Her delicious aroma floated all around him.

There *was* something that bothered him, however. Something about what she'd said regarding her brother...

"Robin?"

"Hmm?"

He smiled at the drowsy sound of her voice. He thought it very sensual, very desirable.

"Can I ask you a question?"

"Sure," she said softly.

"What did you mean earlier when you said you'd waited too long to get to know Jeff?"

At the mention of her brother's name, she stiffened in his arms and he grew alarmed. "It's okay," he said. "We don't have to talk."

"No," she said, "I want to tell you. I want you to understand."

Her silken cheek slid across his skin a fraction.

"I meant to explain when we were downstairs," she continued, "but...I got so upset that I wasn't able to." She splayed her hand on his stomach. "You see, Jeff was years older than I," she said. "All I remember of him was that he was always going off somewhere. To soccer practice. Or baseball practice. Or out with his buddies—"

He felt rather than saw her grin.

"—and the girls seemed to crawl out of the woodwork. Anyway, I never got to spend much time with him."

Suddenly her voice lowered. "And my parents always seemed...elderly to me. I was born in their twilight years. My dad was sickly. And my mom spent all of her time taking care of him. She was a virtual slave to that man. And I promised myself that when I grew up I was going to do just what Jeff did—I was going to enjoy my life. I was going to be independent. I was going to make damned sure that no one, and I mean no one, relied on me."

Her hand slid higher until it rested on his chest. "So I traveled. All over the place. I never stayed in one place long enough to...get to know anyone."

The life-style sounded kind of lonely to Jonas, who had his mom and dad and his sister, Sara, and her family always close at hand. Until recently, anyway.

"And then Tony came into my life," she whispered. "He's dependent on me for everything. I thought I'd resent it. I thought I'd feel trapped. I was so afraid I wouldn't be able to give him what he needed."

Again, he felt her smile against his arm.

"But I love it," she said. "I love getting his breakfast, and changing his diapers, and taking him places. I love seeing life through his eyes. He's a wonderful little boy." She was quiet a minute. "I love him. And I can show him that by doing things for him, being there for him when he needs me."

She hesitated, and Jonas waited in the silent darkness, knowing she wasn't finished with what she had to say.

"I only wish—" her tone was trembly with suppressed emotion "—Mom, Dad, Jeff, Sara. I only wish I could let them know how I feel."

Jonas rolled over, planting his elbows on either side of her. He stared down into her dark, sad eyes. He understood her now. He understood that the cool exterior she presented to the world was just a facade she had used to protect herself.

But, he realized, she'd learned something during the time she'd spent with her brother's son. She'd learned what family means.

"But now it's too late."

Moisture gathered in her eyes and the sadness he read on her face caused him physical pain.

He kissed her mouth gently. "No more tears tonight, Robin," he said. "No more tears."

She smiled, a keen understanding lighting her gaze.

"No more tears," she agreed, huskily.

And she lifted up to meet his kiss.

He kissed her lips with gentle tenderness then tongued. "Robin?" he said. His voice tense.

She sensed a sweet understanding lighting her gaze.

"Do you care?" she asked faintly.

And she lifted up to meet his kiss.

Chapter Seven

With a bandanna covering her hair, Robin wielded a dust cloth as if it were a weapon, attacking the tabletops and chair legs with a vengeance. She realized just how untidy the house had become when she saw Tony's smeary little fingerprints mingling with the dust on the tables in the family room.

She chuckled as she remembered how, when she'd announced her intentions of housecleaning, Jonas had offered to help her, but she could tell by the look on his face that it was an empty gesture and that he hoped she wouldn't take him up on it. She had let him off the hook by asking him to take Tony on an outing that would occupy him for a few hours, although she was almost certain that, between cleaning this huge house and tending the baby, she was the one who had the easier job.

Lively pop tunes were playing over the radio, and Robin danced around the room as she dusted. She couldn't believe how ... good she felt. She supposed it had a lot to do with the fact that she was resting well every night. Removing the pictures of Jeff and Sara had turned out to be an excellent idea—even though she still experienced pangs of guilt. Now, five days after *the event* had taken place, Tony was crying less and sleeping better.

The event was how Robin had come to think of the first night she'd lost herself in grief, only to be rescued by Jonas. She couldn't help the grin that caused the corner of her mouth to twitch every time she thought of their first night together. And she thought of it often. She couldn't help it.

Jonas had been wonderful to her that night. And he continued to treat her in a gentler way ever since the incident. His kindness took her off guard sometimes, just when she expected him to make some kind of quirky, hurtful remark about something she was doing, he would compliment her, or simply smile at her. She found it unnerving, but nice.

Their days had been going so smoothly that it was...weird. All three of them were getting along so well. She felt as though they were playing house. Jonas the daddy, Robin the mommy and Tony the baby. Yes, the days had been wonderful.

And the nights. The nights had been spent in pure ecstasy. At first Jonas had been shocked when he discovered he'd been the first—that he'd taken her virginity. But she'd assured him this was what she wanted, what she needed.

To think that when she first came to Brenville, she couldn't stand to be near Jonas. Their relationship had evolved so rapidly into...

Into what? she wondered. What exactly was it she felt for him?

Robin stopped polishing the table, staring at her reflection in the glassy surface. Was she in love with Jonas?

The question was startling. She'd never been in love in her life.

How was she to even know what love was?

She nibbled on her cuticle as she pondered the answer.

Well, she guessed love—the special kind of love between a man and woman—would be deeply felt. And it would be shown in little ways. She'd want to do intimate, personal things for her special someone.

Her eyes grew wide. Hadn't she made a point of rising early so that she could prepare the coffee before Jonas came downstairs? And hadn't she already decided that she would dust and vacuum his office today as a little surprise?

She covered her mouth with her hand, her eyes growing even wider. And not only had she ironed all his shirts yesterday, but she'd also whistled a happy tune the whole time she was performing the task.

Dear Lord, she *was* in love with Jonas!

The realization brought with it a deluge of questions. How was this going to change things between them? Would this alter her plans of being Tony's sole guardian? It would have to, wouldn't it? And how would Jonas feel when he discovered how she felt? Even more than that, how did Jonas feel about her?

Apprehension churned in the pit of her belly. What if he didn't feel about her the way she felt about him? Then telling him would only make her vulnerable to him.

Yet, her mind argued, she'd been extremely vulnerable during their first night of lovemaking, and he'd been more than understanding, more than kind. He'd given of himself that night—and every night since—more than she would ever have thought he was able to give.

Yes, the argument grew stronger, he'd slept with her, hadn't he? Didn't that account for something? Didn't that mean he felt something for her?

Come on, Robin, a tiny voice said pointedly, *men are men and women are women, and everyone knows sex meant very different things to males and females. Everyone knows that men do it because...well, because... because it feels good.*

Now, a woman was different. A woman made love with a man because she felt something for him. Something deep, something meaningful. A woman *made* love because she *felt* love.

But—Robin couldn't help but frown as the argumentative side of her brain interrupted—*although you were feeling something deep and meaningful the night you made love with Jonas, you really weren't in love with him.*

Closing her eyes, she inhaled deeply. That was true, she had to admit. She hadn't been in love with Jonas the night they had gone to bed together. But she had needed him terribly. And he had responded to her need in a very wonderful way. He had allowed her to hide from her overwhelming grief for a while. He'd permitted her to lose herself in his warmth—he'd let her rejoice in the fact that he was solid, he was breathing, he was alive.

Yes, Jonas had been good to her. But realizing that she hadn't been in love with him when they'd slept together worried her. Did that fact somehow make her less of a woman?

Well, she loved him now, damn it! Isn't that what really mattered? Isn't that what counted?

But now she had to address the issue of telling him how she felt. Should she or shouldn't she?

It wasn't until she'd eased herself down in the desk chair that she realized she'd come into the room that Jonas used as an office. The faint scent of his woodsy after-shave lingered in the air, and the smell of it caused Robin's blood to pulse. It was strange, what the mere thought of this man did to her.

Suddenly she felt lighthearted. She didn't need to decide right at this moment whether or not to tell him how she felt. There was plenty of time for a decision. There were weeks and weeks yet before Jonas was expecting to conclude their present arrangement.

Right now, she simply wanted to hug to her heart this new and wonderful feeling.

She flicked the cloth across the top of the computer monitor and was shocked by the amount of dust particles that flew into the air.

"How does he work in this environment?" she murmured.

Tugging open a window, she stood back and allowed the warm spring breeze to air out the stuffy room. The curtains blew back and several papers on the desk went sailing through the air and onto the floor.

"Uh-oh," she murmured under her breath. She hurried to close the window a bit and then went around the desk to retrieve the papers.

She wouldn't even have thought of looking at Jonas's work, but the word "motherhood" jumped out at her, catching her attention, and she read the first line of the article. Jonas did have talent, she realized, to hook his readers into delving further into his opinion pieces.

In the few minutes it took her to finish the article, Robin experienced a multitude of emotions—all of them, however, were overshadowed by the pain that stabbed her heart.

Her eyes teared up and her throat closed off until she thought she'd suffocate. It was so blatantly obvious that

Jonas had used her inept attempts to "mother" Tony as fodder to feed his sick, opinionated genius for humiliating people.

Oh, he tried to hide the fact that he'd used her trials and tribulations in his article by focusing on "new mothers," but Robin knew he'd taken full advantage of her early care-giving experiences.

She concentrated on the line he'd written regarding how new mothers often felt as though they were part of a juggling act. Robin remembered telling Jonas that very same thing only last week when Tony wanted his lunch but she still had groceries to put away and then the telephone began ringing off the wall. She'd only been trying to share her feelings with Jonas, and now here he was making her out to be some sort of circus clown. Damn him!

The tears blurring her vision made it hard for her to read his clichéd advice that young women should take the tower of lemons that life gave them and make lemonade. He would *have* to bring up her harrowing first experience at the grocery store in the produce department with Tony. God, was nothing safe from the man?

Jonas might as well have taken the blunt-tipped letter opener there on his desk and stabbed her right in the chest, so great was the pain she felt after reading his opinion of her. And the only real reason his opinion mattered was that she'd just discovered what he'd come to mean to her.

She dropped the paper on top of the clutter of articles, books and newspapers on the desktop. She felt so raw, so torn and tortured, as though he'd taken his words and flayed her with them.

Why? Oh, why would he want to hurt her so badly? Had he only treated her nicely over the past few days to put her off the trail of what he was doing here behind the closed door of his office?

The pain that ripped at her heart was agonizing. She let the tears fall.

After only a few miserable moments of surrender to the excruciating ache inside her, she rested her elbows on the desk. Well, there was one consolation. Jonas didn't know that she loved him. And now he never would.

She'd never allow him to know how much his stupid opinion of her hurt. Never. She'd lost enough of her pride as it was.

No, she'd conceal the wounds he'd caused, she'd keep them from him if it was the last thing she did. And disguising her pain would be easy. She'd simply hide her hurt behind a veil of anger.

He wouldn't be home for a while, she realized. But that was okay. The fiery rage she would level on him would lose none of its heat in the waiting.

As it turned out, it was several hours before she was able to speak her mind to Jonas. He'd returned home with Tony, and to her great satisfaction, he'd noticed right away that something was bothering her. She hadn't lied to him. She'd told him that she had something she wanted to discuss, but that she didn't want to do so in front of the baby.

Consequently Tony had sensed the tension in the air and he'd taken quite a while to wind down enough so that he could go to sleep for the night. But once he was all tucked in, his steady breathing proof that he was in a deep slumber, Robin went straight to her room to get herself ready.

She took her time. She brushed her hair, applied a few strokes of blush. For some odd reason, Robin wanted to look good when she told Jonas off.

Staring into the mirror, she thought that maybe she wanted him to realize what he was going to be missing. But then, he would never understand that he'd missed out on her love, because she had no intention of telling him that particular piece of information.

No, she'd stick to the insult and indignation she felt over being used as material for his newspaper article. By the time she'd finished with him, she thought, he'd gladly offer to rip that particular column to shreds.

Armed with the article she'd taken from his desk, she entered the kitchen ready for battle.

Jonas was sitting at the table reading the evening paper and he looked up as she came through the doorway.

"Okay," he said, "what did I do to upset you?"

Silently she placed the piece of paper on the table and slid it over to him. He frowned as he perused it.

Before he had the chance to come up with some calm words that would excuse his behavior, she accused, "You used me."

His green gaze studied her.

"Jonas, you used me and my experiences with Tony to write that piece." She pointed to the paper on the table.

He blinked once. "Of course I did," he said quietly.

Robin had to admit his response startled her. She'd been expecting a denial, or at least an explanation—some kind of subterfuge to evade responsibility. But no, he'd come right out and blatantly admitted his heinous crime.

She had worked out several strong arguments in her head geared specifically to make him own up to what he'd done, but now she was left feeling . . . deflated and empty.

He *knew* he'd used her, and not only that, he didn't seem to mind that she'd discovered it. Somehow, she felt it would have been better if he'd made some sort of refutation, no matter how small. The fact that she felt humiliated didn't bother him in the least.

Her mouth turned cottony all of a sudden and she felt hot tears prickle her eyelids. She would not cry, damn it!

She would not allow him to see how much she was hurting inside.

She cleared her throat in an attempt to try out her voice before she spoke.

"I appreciate your honesty," she said slowly, "but I hate the fact that you violated..." She let the sentence trail in order to control her emotions. She swallowed. Then, she tried again, "I feel that you shouldn't have used me to..." The lump in her throat made it difficult to get the words out.

"Robin..." He reached out and touched her forearm.

"Don't," she said, jerking away from him.

How she wanted to melt into his arms. How she wanted him to apologize and make all the pain go away. But that could only happen in some kind of fantasy world. This was reality.

If she didn't get angry—no, *furious*—right now, then she would fall to pieces and he'd know how she felt about him, he'd know how she hurt.

"I'm not here to further your career!" Her voice grated hot in her throat. "It was low of you to take my first attempts at caring for Tony and use them to entertain your readers."

"But it's my job to entertain my readers," he said quietly. "I wouldn't keep them if I wasn't entertaining." He glanced down at the article lying on the table. "And as for using you, I did. I have to. I write about life. I write about what I observe. And I've been observing you quite a lot lately."

"But you took what I told you—" she moistened her dry lips "—you took my feelings and experiences and made me look like some bumbling foolish circus clown." A hot tear trailed from her eye and she quickly dashed it from her cheek.

"Robin, you're taking this much too personally," he said. "Where's your sense of humor?"

She could hear the edge of defensiveness in his tone, and she hated it.

"Don't try to turn this around," she told him firmly. "Don't make this out to be my problem. You did this. You used me. And I won't let you—"

"I wrote an opinion article on new mothers," he said, his voice rising an octave. "You were the best example I had to work with. I didn't intend to—"

"You did exactly what you intended to do," she cut in viciously, stirring her anger to protect herself. "You intended to embarrass me, you intended to humiliate me. And you did just that."

"Wait a minute." His dark brows were drawn together. "Don't stand there and tell me that you think I isolated you here. Don't you think the experiences you had with Tony are universal ones? Don't you think every new mother in the world feels that she's juggling thirty different tasks at once?"

"But we're not talking about every woman in the world here, are we?" she asked. "We're talking about me."

She plunked one fist on her hip. "Why didn't you use some of the things that happened to you? Why didn't you mention your experience of being peed on? And you are the one who allowed Tony to stand up in the shopping cart and nearly topple out onto the floor. Why, you can't even give the child a simple bath without getting soaked to the skin. And you were the one who had green beans smashed into his hair, not me." She glared at him. "Why didn't you use any of that for material?"

Even though he tried to suppress it, she saw the small smile that tugged ever so gently at one corner of his mouth.

"Because I'm not a mother."

His quick and simple answer infuriated her.

"Oh, pretty convenient," she said through gritted teeth.

"Besides," he went on, "I plan to use my experiences in a piece about new fathers."

After only a moment of hesitation, she said, "So, I guess you think that makes it okay."

"Makes what okay?" he asked.

"Don't play stupid," she snapped at him. "I won't let you make me look like a fool in your column. I don't want people to pick up the newspaper and read about me—"

"It won't be in the paper."

His quiet tone silenced her. She frowned when she saw him press his lips together, as if he'd given something away he hadn't meant to reveal.

What did he mean? she wondered. He wrote a syndicated column, didn't he?

"Well?" she prodded.

Jonas sighed. He rubbed his forehead with his fingertips. Finally he looked up at her. "I hadn't meant for you to find out."

"Find out what?" Her stomach churned, and she had the worst feeling that she was about to receive bad news.

Again, he sighed. "I signed a book contract just a few days before Sara and Jeff's accident. I've been trying to cram my mornings with producing material for the new book and continuing my newspaper columns."

He was saying something important here, Robin knew. Her eyes narrowed as she tried to figure out just what it was.

"You agreed to working in the mornings," she said, her mind still churning. "If you weren't getting enough time to write, why didn't you tell me?"

"Because you wanted to work, too."

That defensiveness was back in his tone. So was the impulsiveness.

"I decided," he said in a rush, "that it would probably take six to eight months to complete the material for the book. Ten at the most."

Robin felt he'd just given her another piece to the puzzle. She wasn't a stupid woman, why couldn't she make the pieces fit together?

"Eight months," she repeated the words slowly. "Ten at the most." She pushed her bangs back from her forehead. "That's how long you said it would take for us to decide which one of us would be the best guardian for Tony." Her voice was hushed as she said, "You were lying, weren't you?"

He just looked at her.

"You were only using me as a means of finishing your book." She lifted her chin a fraction. "You never meant for me to even be a contender in this bout for the guardianship of Tony, did you?"

Damn the tears that sprang to her eyes!

"Robin—"

"No! Let me talk." She smeared her palm across her eyes in a jerky motion. "It doesn't bother me in the least that you used me. Because you see, Jonas, I had every intention of using you, too. I agreed to come here and live with you, I agreed to our farce of a marriage for the sole purpose of learning to care for Tony. I had no intention of discussing with you who would be Tony's guardian. I *knew* it would be me from the very beginning." Her shoulders squared. "How do you like the sound of that?" She raised her brows in question. "How do *you* like being used?"

Before he could answer, she said quickly, "What does bother me is that you thought I couldn't handle being

Tony's guardian. It bothers me more than I can say that you thought I couldn't do the job."

She turned to leave the room.

"Wait."

There was something in his whispered word that stopped her in her tracks. But she kept her back to him.

"Robin, I have to admit that everything you're saying is true. But all of my plans were made before I saw you with Tony."

His tone took on a sort of desperation that made her stop breathing as she waited to hear what he would say next.

"I only thought I was doing what Sara would want me to do," he quickly added.

She turned then. "What do you mean?" Her question was sharp. "Sara didn't want the same thing that Jeff wanted?"

"Of course she did," he said. "I didn't mean anything. I shouldn't have said anything."

"What did you mean?" There was hysteria in her voice and her hands were trembling as she grasped Jonas's arm. "Tell me," she demanded.

His energy seemed sapped and his shoulders rounded. He sighed.

"There were some things Sara said to me," he said evasively. "Things that led me to believe that she felt you ... wouldn't be the best person to raise her son."

Robin couldn't believe her ears. The pain of Jonas humiliating her in his article was nothing next to the ache that ripped through her at this moment. Her sister-in-law didn't believe she could take care of Tony.

"Why did she sign the papers then?" Her voice sounded tinny and wounded, even to her own ears. "Why would she agree to—"

Jonas stood and cupped his palms on her shoulders. "She didn't know you very well, Robin. She said those things to me never having had the chance to see you with Tony. I've seen how you've tried. I've been there as you've—"

"And I thought all along that we were doing what they wanted." Robin felt as though she were in some slow-motion dream. Her throat felt parched and scratchy. Her eye sockets felt gritty, dry. She hurt so bad. So bad, she couldn't even cry.

"We are," he said.

But his assurance fell on deaf ears.

He gave her a gentle shake. "Robin, we're doing exactly what they wanted. We're taking care of Tony. Together."

"But haven't you learned that we can't do it together?" She shook his hands from her. "You use me, I use you..." She reached around him and snatched up his article. "You humiliate me..." She waved the paper under his nose as she said the words. "I can't trust you."

"I didn't do anything wrong," he said, his tone tense.

"Right."

The small muscle at the back of his jaw worked with agitation. Finally he said, "It may have been inappropriate of me not to tell you about the book contract. And I should have told you up front that I intended to remain Tony's guardian." His dark brows drew together. "But where the article is concerned, I did nothing wrong. If you read it again, you'll see that I was only trying to help young mothers. Yes, I was also trying to be entertaining. But I only wanted to let them know that they're not alone in what they're experiencing, and that a lighthearted attitude will keep them from going—" he seemed to search the air for a word "—insane."

He stared at her a moment, frustration and irritation clearly showing on his features. "And if you had even the smallest sense of humor you'd see that what I'm saying is the truth."

With that he turned on his heel and left her standing in the middle of the kitchen.

"Damn the man!" she murmured viciously. She had wanted to be the one who walked out. She had wanted to be the one who left him feeling all alone.

Chapter Eight

"Give me another block," Robin told Tony.

The toddler bent to retrieve a red block from the pile on the floor and then handed it to her.

Carefully Robin placed the block on top of the tower she'd built for her nephew.

"There," she said with a sigh. *"Ta-daa."* She drew her arms wide, drawing his full attention to her presentation.

Tony laughed and clapped, and then, with his eyes twinkling merrily, he took great pleasure in promptly knocking over the tower.

Robin feigned surprise and he laughed louder.

It was a game the two of them played often.

"Paint," Tony demanded.

"You want to finger-paint?" she asked.

His little head bobbed up and down.

"Okay," she agreed easily. "But we have to pick up all the blocks first."

"No."

She tried not to smile as she watched him shake his head emphatically. That small word seemed to have become his favorite lately. She was happy knowing that he felt comfortable enough with her to make demands, and even though it would probably be easier to clean up the blocks herself, she didn't think she should let herself be manipulated by the little imp.

"Well," she told him, "we can't get out the paints until we pick up the blocks."

His bottom lip stuck out stubbornly.

Robin knew she had two choices: she could become obstinate herself, or she could make the chore a game.

"I know—" she kept her tone bright "—let's pick up all the blue blocks first."

She moved the large, round tin closer to the pile of blocks.

"Can you find the blue blocks?" she asked.

Tony's eyes glittered, captured by the idea of a new game. He snatched up a block indiscriminately and offered it to her.

"No," Robin gently told him. "That one's green." She picked up a triangular-shaped one. "This one is blue."

She handed it to him and he plunked it into the metal can. Robin clapped for him and he looked expectantly at her.

"Here's another one," she said. "Now, you find one."

It didn't surprise her when Tony picked up a blue block. They had played this game before, too, and it amazed her how quickly he was learning his colors. Discovering the world with Tony was allowing her see everything with new eyes, and she was learning that the world around her was an awe-inspiring place. And allowing herself to get lost in her time with Tony helped her to forget, at least for a small while, the chaotic turmoil that had made a home in her mind ever since her terrible argument with Jonas.

Soon, the blocks were in the tin and she let Tony place the lid on with a *plunk*.

He scurried into the kitchen, struggled to pull out the heavy kitchen chair and climbed up onto it. He slapped his hands playfully on the tabletop.

"Paint!"

"Okay." Robin laughed.

She got out the little jars of finger paint and a large sheet of heavy paper. The first time she'd painted with him she'd used the thin paper that had come with the kit, and Tony had globbed so much paint onto the paper that it hadn't held up. She'd quickly learned that poster board was worth its weight in gold when it came to finger painting.

After rolling up Tony's sleeves and tying the strings of a smock around his middle, she let him create a painting. He squeezed the thick paint through his fingers, obviously delighted by the slick wetness. The fun he was having made her smile, and soon she joined him, painting an image of her own.

She was outlining the top of a large tree when Jonas walked into the kitchen.

Immediately the air in the room seemed to cool several degrees. He didn't speak to her or Tony, rather he went to the refrigerator and pulled out a bottle of juice. Crossing the kitchen, he opened the cabinet and took out a glass.

"Unka," shouted Tony, obviously affronted that Jonas hadn't acknowledged him when he first came into the room.

Robin saw the tension on the toddler's face. Tony had sensed the change in his new "family." He'd barely had time to get used to his aunt and uncle, and now the uneasiness that always came when they were all together left him once again insecure and apprehensive. It broke Robin's heart to see the question and anxiety in her nephew's eyes. She wished she could do something to relieve it. But she couldn't. The things that had been said between her and Jonas couldn't be taken back.

"That's a beautiful picture, Tony," Jonas said.

He leaned over the child and examined the colorful mess Tony had made on the poster board.

She inhaled the clean, male scent of him, and her heart pummeled her rib cage. Damn! Why did she allow the man to do this to her?

During the three days since they had had their argument concerning his article, they had barely spoken to each other. But every time he came near her, her body reacted. Her heart rate accelerated, her breathing quickened, her whole body would feel flushed. And she fought to hide her physical response.

Just ignore him, she told herself. *Just as he's ignoring you.*

She fully intended to listen to that silent voice inside her head, but then Tony turned his anxious gaze on her.

"Bob-in?"

He reached out his paint-coated fingers to her, and she knew he needed some reassurance.

"It's okay," she said, taking his slippery fingers in hers. The yellow paint on his fingertips mingled with the green on her own.

Then she forced herself to look up at Jonas. *This is for Tony,* she thought sternly. She plastered a smile on her face. "Jonas, are you finished working for the day?" she asked.

"Nope. Just taking a break." His tone was dull and lifeless and he didn't even look at her as he answered her question. He took a swallow of his orange juice as he waltzed out of the kitchen.

A cold chill ran up Robin's spine, forcing her shoulders to square. Her eyes narrowed, but when she felt Tony's questioning gaze on her again, she pulled her lips into what she hoped was a reassuring smile.

Jonas entered the office, a dense cloud of dark emotion following close over his head. He wanted to close the door completely. He wanted to shut himself off from Robin and all the chaos she conjured in him. But he couldn't.

Tony wasn't comfortable with closed doors. Jonas knew his nephew's security was still a fragile thing. So fragile that Jonas didn't want to do anything that might threaten the child's sense of safety.

Leaving the door slightly ajar, Jonas did, however, move to the far side of the room. He stared out the window with unseeing eyes.

He had no idea what to do about the situation between himself and Robin. The woman could make him so angry. The way she had insisted on refusing to see his side regarding the article he'd written. She'd contended that he'd meant to hurt her—personally.

Of course, that was entirely untrue. However, Robin refused to even try to understand his point of view. It was her lack of any sense of humor that was the problem, he knew. The woman simply couldn't laugh at herself, or the situation they were in.

As he gazed out over the side yard, he couldn't keep his mind from drifting to the nights he'd spent with Robin—those hot, passion-filled nights.

Robin had satisfied him in a way he'd never been satisfied. He'd guessed that it had been because of the way she'd so desperately needed him. The first night they had made love, he'd silently questioned whether or not they were doing the right thing, but there had been a pleading in her voice that had been his undoing.

She'd made him feel strong and virile, as though he were the only man alive who could give her what she needed. God, just thinking about it brought a dull, needful ache of his own deep in his loins.

When he'd found out he'd taken her virginity he'd been upset, feeling he'd stolen the special gift she'd been saving for that extra-special someone she would eventually meet. But Robin had been adamant that this was what she wanted. He still marveled at the way she celebrated their coming together. The fervor with which she'd come to him, night after night, had awed him. He loved her excitement. Her enthusiastic passion.

The sight of her pale skin lit by soft moonlight, the flowery scent of her, the satiny feel of her flesh on his, the honey-sweet taste of her lips and those other dark, mysterious places of her supple body he'd kissed . . . The fact that he was the only man who had touched her only made him want her more. He was going to go crazy if—

No, he told himself. The next move was Robin's. He'd simply have to wait patiently until she decided what it was she wanted to do.

He whispered a harsh curse under his breath. Patience wasn't something he seemed to have a lot of right now.

The ceiling of her room was stark white in the bright light of early afternoon. She'd stared at it until her eye sockets felt dry and irritated. She was so confused by all the feelings that warred inside her. With Tony asleep, she had a couple of hours of peace to mull over her emotions.

She was furious at herself for falling in love with a man who cared only for himself and his writing career. He'd used her as a baby-sitter just to—

A voice inside her forced her to stop. She couldn't be angry at Jonas for using her. Not when she'd done the same to him. And she'd used him in more ways than one. She'd used him as support as she learned to care for Tony, and she continued to do so. She'd also used him to get herself through a night that could have been filled with horrible grief—instead, Jonas had turned it into a night of passion, a night of...

"Okay," she whispered aloud. "Okay, already. So I can't be angry that he was using me to take care of Tony."

She'd gone over this a hundred times in her head. And even though she knew it wasn't fair of her to be upset with him, she still wanted to feel that anger. That way she didn't have to focus on the hurt.

These past three days her heart had ached with such pain that she thought surely it would crumble in her chest. Why? she wondered. Why did he have to make fun of her? Why did he have to laugh and jeer when she'd only been trying to do her best? Why did she have to find out about the things Sara had said?

When her sister-in-law came to mind, she purposefully closed the door on those thoughts. Robin found it too torturous to deal with them. She needed to focus on Jonas, she needed to untangle her feelings where he was concerned.

She had started to reread his article on several occasions over the past few days, but each time the humiliation she felt made it impossible for her to get past the first couple of paragraphs. In each instance, she'd had to force herself not to crumple the paper into a ball and fling it from her.

But she sat up on the edge of the mattress now and concentrated on the words. She was going to make herself read his work again. She needed to know if there was even a glimmer of truth to his words when he'd said her experiences were universal and he'd only been trying to help new mothers.

So, setting all emotion aside, she read.

After she finished, she slowly lowered her hand and placed the neatly typed paper on her nightstand. She sighed. As much as she hated to admit it, she could see how a woman, new to motherhood, might find comfort in knowing that she wasn't alone in the catastrophes she experienced in her day-to-day life with a young child.

She put her elbow on her knee and rested her chin on her fist. Jonas had insisted that if she reread his article she'd see his true intent, and now she thought that...maybe she did.

Did that mean he was right about the other things he'd said? Did that mean she had taken his opinion too seriously, too personally?

Maybe from his point of view she had, but then he didn't have a clue how she was looking at it—from the eyes of someone who had fallen in love and then had been immediately disillusioned. She hated the thought of him seeing her as anything other than intelligent and capable, hated that he saw her as inept and uncertain. But then, all new mothers had to feel inept and uncertain at times.

She heaved another sigh. Okay, so Jonas had a point when he said she'd taken the article too personally. She understood his point of view. He didn't have to see things from her side—in fact, she preferred that he didn't, because then he might discover how she felt about him.

Little Tony's face flashed through her mind. She and Jonas had to do something about the icy atmosphere between them. The baby sensed it and was affected by it. She and Jonas had to talk.

Robin rose from the bed and moved toward the door, but as she grasped the doorknob, another thought struck— if Jonas had been right about her lack of a sense of humor, had he also been right about Sara's opinion of her?

Jonas hadn't meant to tell her that Sara thought she wasn't capable of raising Tony, Robin knew that. The way the two of them had flung the angry words around, it was a wonder other things hadn't been revealed—such as the love she felt for him. But as soon as he'd blurted out Sara's thoughts, he'd quickly stressed that she'd made them before ever really knowing Robin.

Robin realized that Sara had never gotten to know her. She also understood that it wasn't Sara's fault. Robin was the one to blame. She'd been too focused on running toward independence and freedom. Too focused on being her own person.

So it was *her* fault that Sara didn't know she could be fully capable of caring for little Tony. And Robin realized that, although she felt hurt by Sara's opinion, she'd had it in her power to change how Sara felt, but she hadn't. And now it was too late.

Smoothing her fingertips across the bedspread, she felt the emptiness inside her grow. It saddened her to think that there was nothing she could do to make amends with her sister-in-law. There was no way for her to go back in time and live her life all over again. She'd simply have to learn to live with this barrenness she felt.

She raised her head, tipping her chin upward. Now, she realized, she needed to deal with the here and now. Right now, it was imperative that she iron out her differences with Jonas. The tension between them was too much for Tony.

Turning the doorknob, she pulled open the door and went in search of Jonas.

He was just closing the front door as she descended the staircase. Robin couldn't read the look in his eyes as he gazed at her.

"This was just delivered for you with the mail," he said.

The envelope was oversize and stuffed full. She knew it would never have fit into the mailbox, which meant the carrier had come to the door. Her problems had so engrossed her that she hadn't even heard the bell.

"Thanks," she told him.

"Looks like it's from your magazine."

She nodded. "I finished up my article. Sent it in days ago." She clasped the envelope to her chest. "And when I called to tell them I couldn't travel anymore, my editor offered me this." She gave a quick glance downward. "They want me to read these articles. They've been submitted by free-lancers. If I think the work has merit, I'm to pass it on to them. Otherwise, I write a rejection."

Jonas bobbed his head slowly. "And you think you can be happy without the travel?"

Would she ever! she wanted to shout. If she could, she would take things back to the way they were before she and Jonas had argued. She'd continue to play house, continue to play the role of wife and mother. And she'd work on slowly changing her role from playacting to the real thing.

Her whole body froze. Where in the world had that thought come from? She might have discovered that her own feelings for Jonas had gone through some kind of metamorphosis, but the deep emotion she felt for him certainly wasn't reciprocated. She could tell by the way he treated her lately, by the way he looked at her. Robin was certain that Jonas was counting the days until he could be rid of her.

Yes, her time with him was slowly but surely ticking away, and turning their relationship into something more than it was right now was impossible. She knew that. All she could hope to do now was thaw out the chilly atmosphere that continued to surround them, maybe get back on friendly terms.

She realized his gaze had narrowed.

"What?" she asked.

He chuckled, and Robin's heart lurched in her chest. She'd come to love the sound of his laugh.

"Well, you must have gotten lost in your thoughts," he said. "Because I had asked you if you'd be happy staying at home."

"Oh, right," she said, flushing when she remembered his question. "I think so," was all she said.

After the length of two heartbeats, he said, "It was good of your editors to find you some work that you can do from here."

"It was."

The awkwardness pulsed between them as if it were a living being. And Robin hated it with a passion.

"Well, then," he said quietly, "congratulations." Again, he gave a vague nod and then took the rest of the mail with him down the hallway. Robin followed close on his heels.

"Can we talk, Jonas?" she asked.

When he didn't stop or acknowledge her in any way, she followed him right straight through the kitchen, where she tossed her fat envelope onto the table. She trailed him into the family room and through the doorway of his office. It was funny how her brother's work space had so easily become Jonas's office in her mind.

He didn't speak to her until he'd rounded his desk and sat down in his chair.

"I don't want to argue anymore, Robin."

There was a hint of pleading in his clear green gaze. And something else, too, she noticed, but she couldn't quite put a name to what she saw there in the set of his jaw.

"I don't, either," she said.

His brows rose in query, and she could tell he didn't believe her.

"I didn't come in here to fight with you," she assured him.

He didn't speak; he simply leaned back in his chair and waited.

A sudden case of nerves had her rubbing and pressing the thumb of one hand into the palm of the other. She could kick herself for not planning what she'd meant to say, for now it seemed that no words would come.

She looked down at her hands, and then out the window as she stalled for time. Time in which to compose some kind of speech.

Tipping up her chin, she steeled herself to start the conversation.

"I came," she began slowly, "to talk about us." She waved her hand to indicate the two of them. "Things have changed since our...argument."

She looked at him. He gazed at her, his eyes shuttered, unreadable.

Finally he commented, "You expected our relationship to remain the same after the things we said to each other?"

"But this—" she hesitated "—this coldness between us isn't good for Tony. It frightens him."

"Yeah, well it's a cold, cruel world out there. Maybe the sooner he finds that out, the better."

The bitterness in his voice surprised her. She'd never heard him talk that way before. His laughing and joking might have irritated her in the past, but this harshness was somehow disconcerting.

"Jonas, you don't mean that," she said. "We're supposed to shield him from all the bad stuff life has to offer." Very softly, she added, "That's what guardians do."

The sound that came from him had a derisiveness that kept it from being described as a laugh.

This wasn't going at all as she'd thought, and there was a moment of tense silence before she spoke again.

"I know that when we first agreed to take care of Tony together, we really didn't get along very well." She looked down where her fingers were all knotted together in front of her. "But I felt like that was changing. We were growing closer."

Although she wasn't talking about their lovemaking, the short sentence brought the event to her mind with such vivid clarity that every inch of her skin flamed hot. Her gaze darted to his face, and she could tell he was thinking about the same thing. A wave of mortification hit her with enough force to make her reach out and grasp the edge of the desktop.

She could feel her mouth working, but no sound came out. Finally she stammered, "Well...I... What I mean is—"

"I know exactly what you meant," he said. He leaned back in his chair, his voice steady as he commented, "I know you weren't talking about our being together, but I don't like to think you're flustered or embarrassed about what happened between us. You took comfort in me, and I took comfort in you. It's as simple as that."

His tone was flat, but the man did have a way with words. And she was grateful that he summed up how they should feel about what happened to them in such a neat, tidy little package.

"But you do have to admit," he continued, "that our nights together were the catalyst that changed our relationship for the better. Once we slept together, we began treating each other with a little more...consideration, a little more kindness."

She felt uneasy following the path this conversation had suddenly taken and tried to veer into another direction.

"And getting back to that place," she said, "where we treated each other...kindly—that's what I'm interested in."

A glimmer came to his eye, but she sensed an impulsive spark of maliciousness there that put her on her guard.

"So," he said flippantly, "you want to spend more nights comforting each other?"

"Of course I don't!" she snapped.

Before she realized it, he'd pushed himself from his chair, rounded the desk and grasped her upper arms in his strong hands.

"Are you sure?" The three short words he whispered were harsh and taunting. "We were so good together."

Robin was stunned silent. They *had* been good together, and she'd loved the nights she'd spent in his arms. But there was so much anger and bitterness in his tone.

Her eyes widened when he covered her mouth with his.

His kiss was hard, and rough. And it felt like heaven to taste him again.

Robin lowered her eyelids, and reveled in the feel of his lips on hers, in the taste of his tongue when he deepened the kiss. His hands slid along her back and pulled her close.

He smelled so good, tasted so good, felt so good. Her hands rose almost of their own volition, sliding behind his neck, her fingers entwining in his silky hair.

Despite the fury coursing through him, Jonas could feel himself being carried away by the pure enjoyment he felt in Robin's closeness. He hadn't realized just how much he'd missed the physical part of their relationship over the past few days.

The luscious, hot taste of her on his tongue sparked a desire deep inside him that throbbed with a heavy, fiery beat. He wanted desperately to lose himself in her. But he couldn't allow that to happen.

He was angry. Yes, he was so damned angry that he couldn't see straight. He'd known that she'd used him, that he'd used her, but saying the words, hearing them spoken out loud had made him furious. He'd wanted so much more, he realized. He'd wanted Robin to love him. Like he loved her. But it was so obvious that she just didn't feel that way.

The thought had enraged him for some reason. Had enraged him to the point that he'd rushed at her, had forced himself on her. He should be appalled by his actions. Yet, here he was continuing his assault.

He pulled back a scant fraction of an inch, just enough to whisper her name against her swollen lips. Shame and embarrassment welled up inside of him as he looked down into her beautiful face. Thank God her eyes were closed.

However, they weren't closed for long.

He watched her lids rise, slowly, almost languidly, and for a moment, he allowed hope to spring up inside of him. Maybe, he thought, this kiss could be the catalyst that brought them together. But the instant of confidence was dashed when he saw the coldness in her gaze—a coldness that froze him to the core.

Well, she wouldn't know how he hurt. Never in a million years. "See?" he said before she had a chance to speak. "See how good we are together?"

Robin knew Jonas was hedging for a fight, even though he'd voiced otherwise when she'd first entered the office. She squared her shoulders and tipped up her chin, refusing to give him the argument he was looking for.

"Damn it, Jonas," she said, feeling her throat swell with distress. "I came in here to apologize for the things I said when we argued. I came in here hoping to smooth things over with you because I think the way we've been treating each other is affecting Tony. We should try to get along. For Tony's sake."

"For Tony's sake," he repeated, stepping away from her.

The dullness had returned to his voice.

"Yes," she said, trying hard to regain her composure.

His face gave away none of his feelings. "So, what you're saying is that you want us to be nice to each other."

"Exactly."

Now we are getting somewhere, she thought, *if I could only forget that kiss ever happened.*

"Even though," he went on, "so much has happened between us? We've made love—" He gave a disgusted snort. "Let me rephrase that, we've had sex. We've revealed to each other that each of us had been blatantly using the other. And you've made it quite clear that you feel my work isn't worth the paper it's written on." His dark brows rose as he asked, "And you want us to pretend to be friends?"

There was incredulity in his question. As she saw it, she had two ways to go here. She could lambaste him with the irritation and frustration he stirred up in her—an irritation and frustration he seemed hell-bent on stirring up. Or she could remain calm.

In the end, she decided calm was the best method.

"Jonas, I respect your work," she said. "It may not be my choice of reading material, but I respect what you do. Okay?"

He didn't even blink in response.

"And as for you using me and me using you..." She bit her bottom lip for a split second as she chose her words. "That's all in the past. We need to get beyond it."

He ran his fingers along the length of his strong jaw. "No matter how hard we try to get beyond it, the past always affects the future. What does the future hold for us, Robin? What's going to happen in the weeks and months ahead?"

They were legitimate questions, ones she'd spent hours puzzling over lately.

"I don't know," she answered him honestly. "I can't say what tomorrow will bring. I don't know what my plans are. All I do know is that I love Tony. And I know you do, too. And the two of us will have to take that into consideration in whatever actions we decide to take."

Now he folded his arms across his chest and he seemed to press his back against the chair in an effort to get as far away from her as he could. He was distancing himself from her, and it made her feel more alone than she'd ever felt in her life.

"I will promise you, though," she told him quietly, "that I'll be honest and up-front about my plans. Whenever I finally make them."

She'd hoped that he'd reciprocate that promise, but when he didn't, she silently turned and walked out of the room.

Robin went into the kitchen. She filled a mug with water and put it into the microwave to heat. As she took a tea bag from the box, she thought about what a mess this coguardianship had turned out to be.

"Robin!"

There was a quality in Jonas's voice when he called out to her that had her heart racing. She rushed across the kitchen.

Maybe he'd decided to forgive her for the things she'd said during their argument. Maybe he'd come to understand the need for a better relationship between the two of them for Tony's sake.

She poked her head into his office, leaning heavily on the doorjamb. What she saw infuriated her. The man hadn't even taken the time to think on their discussion. Evidently he thought so little of the things she'd said that he'd immediately put her request for a friendlier relationship out of his head and turned to the task of opening the day's mail. He sat now with his head bent over one particular letter. She still couldn't believe how easily he could aggravate her. Damn, but the man could infuriate her with the smallest amount of effort on his part.

But when he looked up at her, there was something in his green gaze that caused her breath to catch in her throat.

"I think," he said quietly, "we may be in trouble."

Chapter Nine

He seemed to stare right through her. Then his gaze dropped back down to the paper he held in his hand and he scanned the letter.

Silent seconds throbbed by. She could stand the tension no longer. "What?" she asked.

When he didn't answer immediately, the anxiety that coursed through Robin sharpened her tone as she asked, "What is it, Jonas?"

His eyes leveled on her again.

"This letter is from my lawyer," he said. Then he corrected, "*Our* lawyer."

The frown planted firmly between his brows sent apprehension flashing through her like a bolt of lightning.

"It seems that the insurance company that insured the cabin wants to settle," he said.

"You mean the cabin where Jeff and Sara...died?" The question stuck in her throat.

"Yes," he said.

The news had her a bit confused. She stepped farther into the room. "But isn't that a good thing?"

"It is."

But the fact that the anxiety didn't leave his face filled her with dark dread.

"Well, then I don't understand—"

"It seems the insurance company," Jonas said, plowing ahead, "is going to make Tony a very rich little boy."

She paused. Jonas seemed to be delivering information that should make him happy. But the concern evident in his countenance caused her bewilderment to increase.

"Our nephew will want for nothing for the rest of his life," Jonas said.

The look in his eyes was grave, and Robin felt her hands begin to tremble. Something was coming, something bad. She could feel it in her bones.

"Would you explain what's going on?" she pleaded. "Why are you so...upset over what should be good news?"

He inhaled deeply and raked his fingers through his collar-length hair. Robin realized that, during the many days that she'd been living in the house with him, he'd never taken the time to have his hair cut—she also realized she liked it just the way it was.

"The judge wants a progress report."

Even though his voice was quiet, each word seemed to explode like a stick of dynamite.

"A progress report?" She felt her mouth go dry. "But why?"

"Well, isn't it obvious?" He slapped at the letter lightly. "Tony's going to come into a lot of money."

"But why should that have anything to do with the judge? We were granted custody. We're Tony's aunt and uncle." After only a moment's hesitation, she added, "And besides all that, we're married."

"And under what circumstances did we marry, Robin?" he asked.

When she opened her mouth to answer, he stopped her by raising his hand, palm side out.

"Allow me," he said. "We married so we would be granted custody. And now Tony's going to be rich . . ."

She gasped at the implication. "But we didn't do it for the money!"

"You know that, and I know that—" he raised his brow "—but do you honestly think that the judge will believe it? Can you look the woman in the eye and tell her you didn't expect your nephew to be awarded compensation for the accidental death of both his parents?"

Her tone was weak as she replied, "I never thought about it . . . I never knew . . ."

"Yes, you did," he said. "I told you right up front that I was having my lawyer pursue the matter."

Jonas's words jogged her memory. She remembered telling him that no amount of money would take the place of Jeff and Sara.

"But what can the judge do?" she asked. "Like I said before, we're married."

"But we didn't marry for love," he said.

The derisiveness in his tone made her want to flinch.

"We didn't even marry with Tony's best interests in mind. We married for our own selfish reasons." He tossed the letter onto the desk. "Try explaining that to the judge and see how much sympathy you'll get."

Robin swallowed. "We could lie. We could say we married for love." It was an irrational thought, she knew, but she was suddenly feeling scared to death.

Jonas shook his head. "All the judge would have to do is talk to that young court clerk. What was her name? Anita? Alice? Whatever. She'd remember how we reacted to each other." Then he hissed. "She'd probably even admit she was the one who planted the idea of marriage in our heads to begin with. God, what a mess."

She lowered herself into the padded, high-back chair near the desk. "Maybe we didn't marry under the best of circumstances, but why should that matter? Tony doesn't have any other family besides us. I mean, your mom is busy caring for your father. He's only got you and me to look after him."

Robin felt as though she was thinking aloud, and she didn't much like where her thoughts were going. Finally, when the crux of the matter formed as words in her head, her eyes widened.

"They couldn't take him away from us, could they?"

There was foreboding in Jonas's eyes, in his face, in the silent language of his body.

"Tony's going to be wealthy," he said. "Very wealthy. And I'm sure you've heard the phrase 'money is power.' Maybe the courts wouldn't give him to someone else—but they might make us decide who he should be with—you or me. Someone would have to be in charge of his sizable account."

"Dear God." Robin barely heard her whispered words as blood whooshed through her ears. Her heart rate accelerated and she felt nervous perspiration prickle across her skin. Was that where she and Jonas were headed? she wondered. On opposite sides of a custody battle?

She didn't like the thought. Not at all.

"I wouldn't take you to court over Tony." But even as the words were leaving her mouth, she couldn't help but wonder if they were true.

It wasn't about the money—that issue held no real meaning for her. She loved her nephew. And she'd come to love taking care of him. Feeding him. Calming his fears. Kissing his boo-boos. Laughing at his innocent antics. She wanted to spend the next twenty years raising him into a man her brother would have been proud of. And suddenly she realized that she'd fight heaven and earth to get the chance to do it.

Her gaze slid from his, and she stared at her hands where they were clasped tightly in her lap.

"I'm almost glad you don't mean it," Jonas said quietly. "It shows that you've acquired a protective... motherly instinct. An instinct that has proved Sara wrong."

She could almost hear a tiny smile in his words, a kind of... affection. But when she looked up at him, his eyes held some intense, unreadable emotion, as though he was experiencing an overwhelming anguish that he couldn't express.

Well, she knew exactly how he felt. And she wanted to reach across the desk and touch his hand. She wanted to let him know she understood. But she didn't. There was some huge, invisible wall that stood in her way.

"Listen," he said, "we're supposed to have a meeting with the lawyer on Monday. I'll call Amy and ask her to keep an eye on Tony. I don't want you to worry about this."

There was an intensity in his green eyes—an intensity she'd never seen before.

"We'll straighten this out," he went on. "I'll make everything okay."

She nodded, but she knew that nothing he could say would calm the fear that was gnawing her alive.

* * *

Robin closed the door of his office as she left, and Jonas sat there feeling cold and empty and utterly alone. This farce of a marriage had twisted and turned his emotions until he didn't know what he felt anymore.

When he'd pushed Robin to become his wife, he had to admit, he'd done it with no one else in mind but himself. Yes, his conscience had tweaked him, but he'd ignored the guilt, feeling that the end justified the means. He realized he was wrong not to have been totally honest with her. But then she hadn't been honest with him, either. Hell, he guessed that he and Robin deserved each other. He wondered, if he could turn back time, would he make the same choices?

Granted, this time with Robin had been like a fast-moving amusement park ride—a harrowing yet eye-opening experience. And one he didn't think he would want to pass up, even if he could.

He'd gone into this relationship believing Robin to be a selfish woman who only thought of her career. However, he'd discovered things about her. Things about her character. About her background. Things that he'd found endearing.

As the days passed, he saw how hard Robin tried to give Tony all the love and care that Sara would have wanted her son to have. He'd witnessed the terrible pain she'd felt over Tony's initial rejection of her. He'd watched her strive to win the baby's trust, and he knew she felt relieved and grateful when she discovered she finally had it.

Sure, Robin had made mistakes. He thought back over the days and weeks since they took on the job of coguardianship. He remembered when she'd tried to feed Tony cooked carrots and the baby had tossed each round piece to the floor. He smiled when he thought of the first time she'd washed Tony's face and she'd gotten a little soap in his eyes. Tony had cried and Robin's own eyes had welled with tears as she apologized to him profusely. Yes, she'd made her mistakes. But then, Jonas knew he'd made plenty of those himself.

He couldn't believe how well they had worked together as a team from the very beginning—especially when they really didn't seem to like each other very much. Of course, he realized now that each of them had come to their negative opinions of the other before they'd really gotten to know each other.

His early conclusions concerning her character had been quickly and easily proved wrong, and he realized that he and Sara hadn't really been fair to Robin. She'd had her reasons for staying away, and she felt a terrible guilt now that she saw what she'd missed out on by not visiting her family.

The ultimate turning point of his emotions, he knew, was the first night they had spent together. Yes, before that point, he did admit that his opinion of her had been slowly changing and her dedication to Tony had impressed him. But his image of her as cool and distant remained firm in his head. Until he'd slept with her.

As he'd held Robin in his arms and soothed her tears, he'd come to realize that she had her fair share of vulnerability. He'd learned that underneath that thin veil of remoteness that she put on as a way of proving her independence, there was a warm and susceptible woman—a woman who was willing to give of herself—a woman who was not afraid to take what she needed.

Jonas had been absolutely joyous to have had the chance to meet that woman. He'd cherish the memory of her in his heart forever. And it was for that memory—for that woman—that he felt an overwhelming desire to fix this situation.

He wished things could have turned out differently for them. He wished...

Pushing the useless thought aside, he thought back, instead, on the irrational anger he'd felt when Robin had come to him just now to patch up their relationship. The animosity that had coursed through him had been a blanket disguising deeper, more complex emotions. So he'd allowed his irritation at her apology to surface in the form of cutting remarks and a vicious kiss.

No, he told himself, it really hadn't been her apology that bothered him, it had been her motivation. She'd sought to smooth out the rough spot between them "for Tony's sake." The sound of her voice echoed in his head and he suffered through a shiver of cold ire...no, it was some other unnameable emotion that vibrated along his spine.

Jonas had hoped that she'd come to see him to work things out because...well, because she'd wanted to work things out for herself. And for him.

He had wanted to go to her during the days since their argument. He had wanted to explain once again that he hadn't meant her any harm. He'd long since decided not to use the piece he'd written on motherhood, and he'd wanted to tell her that, too. But he had come to learn how stubborn she could be—just as stubborn as he was himself. Jonas couldn't stop the smile that quirked one corner of his mouth.

She wouldn't have listened to a word he'd have to say. No, Robin needed to come to terms with her anger on her own. And she had, he'd learned. She'd obviously decided that she didn't want to have anything more to do with him, on a personal level. But she felt she needed to alleviate the tension between them "for Tony's sake."

Jonas found himself gritting his teeth. He'd wanted the situation to be resolved in a manner that would allow their relationship to progress to a more personal—a more intimate level. And his longing for that kind of resolution and progression was spurred, he knew, by the true woman in Robin he'd come to know. The woman he'd come to desire.

He rubbed his eye sockets, unable to clear from his mind the dreamy images that replayed themselves in his head in hot, velvety night fantasies. He made slow, passionate love to the woman every single night.

And he'd spent his days drawing her out from beneath the thick protective mantle that Robin wrapped herself in. He'd succeeded, too. He'd enjoyed the short time he'd had with the easygoing, fun-loving woman who had emerged after they had slept together. But then Robin had discovered his article, and she'd retreated into that rock-hard shell of hers. He missed the woman he'd found. Missed her terribly.

As he sat here at the desk now, he realized that it was for that wonderful woman he'd discovered in Robin that he felt compelled to remedy this custody predicament.

His hand shook a bit as he touched a button that cleared his computer screen. And his gut never once stopped jumping the whole while he composed his letter.

Robin thought this had been the longest weekend of her entire life. Apprehension and worry chewed on her insides like hungry, persistent mice. A dozen questions rolled in her head, keeping restful sleep at bay. Both Friday night and Saturday night had been spent tossing and turning, and when she had slept, her dreams had been filled with heartbreaking images.

The nightmares had been vivid and haunting, crowded with sorrow and tears, congested with anguish.

There had been a couple of different scenarios during her night visions. In one, she had watched Jonas walk away from her with Tony in his arms. She was left feeling empty and aching, her eyes so full of tears she could barely see the baby wave goodbye. In the other, she was the one who cradled Tony protectively, she was the one who walked away, and the excruciating pain on Jonas's face had etched itself in her memory, plaguing her all her waking hours.

She'd spent the days feeling worn-out and nervous. And she'd feared that her tiredness would affect her patience where Tony was concerned. But she quickly found out that was something she never should have worried about. Patience and attention were both very easy things to give to Tony—especially when his future was so clouded and uncertain.

"Hey."

She swiveled her head at the sound of Jonas's voice. He looked just as tired as she felt. She guessed his nights had been as troubled and sleepless as her own. She hoped he understood her commiseration in the smile she offered.

He stepped out onto the back porch to join her in the quiet, silky night. The mere sight of him had her feeling flushed and self-conscious. No matter what happened at the lawyer's office tomorrow morning, no matter what the future held for them both, she could never deny to herself the deep feelings she had for this man.

Jonas held the back screen door open and scooted to one side. Robin's smile widened as she watched Tony emerge from the house.

"Bob-in." He gave her a wide grin, let go of his uncle's finger and toddled toward her.

"You little rascal," she teased, pulling him across her lap and burying her face in his belly.

Tony laughed, loving the way she tickled him.

After a moment, Robin sat him up and said, "I thought you were getting a bath."

She nearly laughed at the guilty expression on Tony's sweet little face.

"Unka," he accused, and pointed a pudgy finger at Jonas.

"Oh—" Jonas chuckled "—so you're going to get me in trouble, huh?"

"Nobody's in trouble," Robin assured them softly.

Jonas eased himself down onto the step next to her. He reached out and grasped Tony's foot, his hand gently grazing her thigh. She wanted badly to close her eyes and enjoy his touch. She might never feel it again.

His solidness so near to her warmed the cool evening air considerably. Slowly, inconspicuously, she inhaled, filling her lungs with the clean, fresh smell of him that mingled so deliciously with his enticing cologne.

He leaned toward Tony and ruffled his curly, red hair, and when he did, his shoulder brushed intimately against hers. She turned her face and saw that his handsome profile was only inches away from her. He kept his eyes on Tony.

"We going to catch us some—"

"Bugs!" Tony barged in on his uncle.

Jonas chuckled, a wonderful sound that had Robin smiling, despite the shudder that ran over her skin upon hearing their plans for the evening.

"I don't have to help, do I?" she asked. "I mean, just the thought of seeing a bug, let alone catching one, has my skin crawling."

Jonas's green gaze glittered with mischief. "Oh," he said, "so you have a phobia with bugs."

Light laughter emanated from deep in his throat, and she felt her insides soften. She wished she could press the flat of her palm against his chest and feel the vibration of it. She pushed the thought aside and focused on the conversation at hand.

"Just a tiny little one," she commented, keeping her tone as light as possible.

"Bugs, bugs," Tony chanted.

He squirmed in an effort to get out into the yard. Afraid he might fall on the concrete steps, Robin carried him onto the grass and then put him down. He staggered his first few steps across the uneven ground, but quickly found his balance.

"We're going after lightning bugs," Jonas said. "Of course, we'll let them go after a while."

It was then that she noticed he had an empty baby food jar in his hand, the lid punctured with holes.

"Lightning bugs? Well, that's different," she said, moving out into the darkness with him. "Lightning bugs are beautiful, not like those other icky creepy crawlers, like spiders and centipedes and..." She shivered.

Jonas took her elbow. "Don't worry," he said, his tone gentle and absolutely serious, "I won't let them get you."

She knew he was teasing her, but as she looked up into his handsome face, it was as if the world stopped turning and in that soft, moonlit moment there was a complete cessation of time. The feeling that welled up in her was strange and strong. She wanted desperately to reach out and touch his cheek. She wanted to kiss his mouth. She wanted to wrap her arms around him and beg him to stay here with her for all the years it would take for Tony to grow into adulthood.

But she didn't. She didn't because she simply couldn't let down her guard long enough to perform the actions and say the words. Besides, it would be an effort in futility. If there was one thing she'd learned during her stay here in Brenville, it was that she and Jonas just couldn't get along together. Sure, they had times of perfect harmony—their moments of passion flashed, unbidden, into her mind with crystal clarity, and she remembered the wonderful days during which they'd gotten along so well—but the dark times always came. She thought about their arguments, their cutting, sarcastic remarks and the harsh, hot kiss. It seemed the two of them were hell-bent on hurting each other.

"Unka!" Tony called out from the back of the yard.

"I'm coming," Jonas called.

He looked at Robin. "Come on. Let's go catch some lightning."

Her breath caught in her throat and she stopped short.

"What?" Jonas asked. "What'd I say?"

"Jeff used to say that," she whispered, her voice suddenly raspy and dry. "Let's go catch some lightning."

Jonas nodded. "Yeah, I've been hunting with Jeff and Tony before."

"No, no," she rushed to say. "I mean, Jeff used to say that to *me.*" Emotion swirled around her, thick and heavy, and she found it hard to breathe. "When I was a little girl," she explained around the lump that had suddenly formed in her throat, "Jeff used to take me out in our backyard and we'd catch lightning."

I remember! It was a revelation. A wonderful revelation. She remembered spending time with her brother as a child. The memory must have been buried under the mound of guilt she'd felt over staying away from her family. And it had been Jonas who had unearthed it.

She sandwiched his face between her hands and planted a firm kiss full on his lips. His eyes grew wide and questioning, and she threw her head back and laughed.

"I'm so happy!" she said, not caring that her voice was loud enough to wake the neighbors. Then she leveled her gaze on him once more. "Thank you, Jonas. Thank you."

He seemed to hover somewhere between wanting to laugh with her and wanting to call the paddy wagon to report her insane.

"I don't know what I did," he said. "But I'm happy to help you out anytime."

Again Robin laughed. There were other memories of Jeff planted deep in her head! She'd hoped and prayed there would be, but she hadn't been sure until now. The realization brought tears of joy to her eyes. All she had to do was excavate them.

She wanted to dance and frolic in the cool spring night. She wanted to share her sudden and unexpected happiness with the whole world. She wanted to sing and shout.

"Come on, Jonas!" she called, tugging on his sleeve. "Let's go catch some lightning."

Chapter Ten

Heavy, gray clouds blanketed the sky. Robin was certain that the threatening storm would break at any moment. It was a perfect day to be tortured by trepidation. A perfect day to be on the way to a meeting that just might change the future in a very bad way.

They had dropped off Tony at Amy's, and Robin and Jonas were now driving slowly along Main Street, casing the curb for a free parking spot.

She cast a sidelong glance at Jonas. His jaw was firmly set and she could read the tension in his rigid features. She wanted to reach out and reassure him, but she simply couldn't. Not when she was so unsure of the outcome of this meeting.

As Jonas steered the car down a narrow side street, Robin took the opportunity to go over the events of last night. The hour or so that she and Jonas and Tony had spent together would ever remain in her mind as a cherished memory.

Without even knowing what he'd done, Jonas had given her a small piece of her brother last night. And from that little piece, she'd decided there must be others that were just waiting to be remembered. The happiness she'd felt had been all-consuming, and it was all because of Jonas.

But what stuck with her, more so than her beautiful revelation about Jeff, was the way Jonas had treated her and Tony last night. Especially Tony. There had been a— she searched for a word to describe his behavior—a *desperation* in his actions. It was as if he was afraid that Tony was going to be snatched away from him at any moment. Jonas seemed to savor his time with his nephew. He had been reluctant to go inside when Robin suggested it was way past Tony's bedtime. Jonas had insisted on being the one to get the baby ready for bed, had insisted on reading him his favorite storybook.

It had been a sad thing to watch, and Robin had tried to come up with some way to smooth over his fears, but she'd failed. She'd failed because she truly understood the fear and anxiety he was experiencing. She felt it, too, and there was nothing that could be said or done that would alleviate that terrible dread that lay heavy in her belly. So she hadn't patronized him by offering him fluffy, empty words of assurance.

Jonas backed into a parking spot and they got out of the car in silence. A tense cloud seemed to hover around them all the way around the block and up the brick steps of the professional building that housed the lawyer's office.

After greeting the secretary with tight-lipped smiles, the two of them sat down on the hard-back chairs in the small, cube-shaped waiting area. Robin could tell that Jonas was just as nervous as she was by the way he flexed and un-flexed his fists, then he smoothed his flattened palms down his thighs, then he weaved his fingers together and plunked his hands onto his lap. Soon he unlaced his fingers and began the sequence all over again: flexing, smoothing and weaving.

Her heart went out to him. Seeing him in such a state of nervous agony only reminded her again how much she'd come to care for him. She loved this man, and she'd do anything to save him from suffering all this uncertainty.

"Mr. Myer will see you now." The secretary's soft voice broke into her troubled thoughts.

Robin felt as though she floated into the inner office. The tenebrous shadows of apprehension wrapped her in a strangling cloak. She opened her mouth and struggled to take a deep breath.

Jonas introduced her to the smartly dressed man standing on the other side of the desk, but Robin's overwrought emotions let the man's name slip right out of her brain like water in a sieve.

Tom Myer, his nameplate pronounced. She stared at the narrow, bronze-colored plate and chanted the man's name over and over, hoping that she could overcome this panic that welled in her with sudden fury. She felt like a volcano that was just about to erupt.

"I want to tell you right away," the lawyer rushed to say. "The insurance company faxed me over the weekend."

Through a thick haze of emotion, Robin sensed that he was extremely excited. She was relieved that he focused his attention on Jonas, because until she could get herself under control, she didn't think she'd be much good at discussing the insurance situation or the legalities of Tony's custody. Absently she reached into her pocket for a tissue.

"Sit, sit," Tom instructed.

The leather underneath her felt cool against her stockinged legs.

"They're anxious to settle," Tom told Jonas. He grinned. "And that means more money for your nephew."

She glanced at Jonas as he nodded at the lawyer, but his jaw muscle remained taut. Tom's conversation seemed to fade into the background as she looked at the man she'd married.

There had been so many things she'd learned about Jonas during their time together. He could be irritatingly witty—in fact that was his great talent, attested by his success as a writer. But she had seen the gentle, kind side of him, too. She twisted the tissue, remembering all the times he had been supportive and giving. And she knew beyond a shadow of a doubt that he loved Tony with all his heart.

She realized in that instant that she could never do anything that would hurt Jonas and Tony—the two men in her life who had captured her heart.

Who did she think she was? she wondered. Did she honestly believe she could come barging into Brenville and take Tony away from the only family he had left? Tony hadn't even remembered her, for God's sake! If it hadn't been for Jonas, the child would probably still be screaming in utter fear of her.

"Just give me a few more weeks," she heard Tom say. "I need more negotiating time."

Robin stared down into her lap, the tissue lay torn to shreds on the fabric of her skirt. She couldn't do this anymore! She couldn't sit here like a meek lamb waiting to be slaughtered. Not when the futures of the two people she loved most in the world seemed to be dangling so precariously.

"I want to talk about this progress report," she blurted.

She hadn't given in to the urge to stand, but she had scooted to the very edge of the smooth leather chair. Fine pieces of the paper tissue fell from her lap to the plush carpet, and she let them fall, unheeded.

The room was so quiet it was eerie. Tom's bushy gray brows rose with the surprise he was obviously feeling. Robin didn't dare look at Jonas, not with what she was about to say.

"Jonas and I are...are having a problem with our marriage." There, the blunt statement was out. She felt a sick sense of relief...as if there was no turning back now that she'd begun.

"Robin."

Jonas's voice held a burr of warning. But she ignored it. She was doing this for his own good.

"I don't think our relationship is going to last," she said to the lawyer. "But I want you to know that Tony will be well cared for."

The pain that knifed through Jonas was nearly physical in its intensity. He would never have guessed that Robin would attack so quickly. He knew she wanted Tony, and he had done what he could to see that she'd get what she wanted. But he was shocked that she couldn't even wait long enough to see that he'd fixed the situation.

Well, he'd go through with his plans. He steeled himself, holding on to a tiny thread of salvation that came in knowing that, once she got what she was looking for, she'd never again be able to hurt him.

"You see," Robin went on, "the magazine I work for said I couldn't keep my job unless I'm willing to travel. And my job is my life."

Jonas frowned in confusion. What was she talking about? *Fancy Food* had been good enough to give her a pile of editing work that she could do from the house.

"I can't imagine being stuck at home with a small child."

She's lying, he realized. He could hear it in the way her voice trembled. But, why? What the hell was she doing?

"Robin," he said, reaching out and touching her forearm.

But she refused to look at him, and when she gruffly brushed off his hand, he became lost in the mire of his confused emotions.

Robin stood up abruptly. She knew that if she didn't say it now, she never would. "I plan on filing for divorce. And I want to sign over custody of Tony to Jonas."

"What the hell?"

Hearing Jonas's outburst, she nearly lowered her guard and turned toward him, but she held firm and stared straight at Tom Myer.

"Well, I'm just a little confused," Tom told her.

"Robin, we need to talk."

"Be quiet, Jonas," she snapped.

Although she didn't see his actions, she could sense the heavy shield he raised against her. She heard the rustle of material as he crossed his arms over his chest.

Tom opened a folder that lay on his desktop. "It seems that we have a mighty big problem here. I received a hand-delivered letter late Friday from Jonas telling me that he, too, has decided against being responsible for Tony. It looks like neither one of you wants the poor child."

"Oh, but I do!" The words gushed from her in a great rush. "But..." She glanced at Jonas's closed-off expression then back at the lawyer. Her tone was weak as she said, "But so does he." She made a feeble motion to point at Jonas as she eased herself back down to sit on the very edge of the seat.

Tom spent several moments looking from Robin to Jonas and back again, his silent questions filling the awkward silence.

"Let me get this straight," Tom said finally, "you two are married, you've been living in the same house, yet neither one of you knows what the other is doing."

Robin looked down and began picking at the pieces of the shredded tissue fibers still stuck to her skirt. She was too embarrassed to look the lawyer in the eye.

Then Jonas spoke. "I guess we owe you some kind of explanation."

The look on Tom's face displayed the opinion that he agreed wholeheartedly.

"You see," Jonas began, "it's all my fault. I coerced Robin into marrying me because I needed help with Tony until I finished the book contract I'd recently signed—"

"But I allowed myself to be coerced." Robin started her spiel overtop of Jonas's words. "I needed Jonas in order to—"

"Hush, Robin," he demanded harshly. "Let me talk."

Jonas, too, was now on the edge of his chair. "You see, Tom, because the judge is concerning himself with the insurance money..."

He hesitated, evidently finding it hard to come up with just the right words to explain.

"We became worried about this progress report," he told the lawyer. "If it's going to jeopardize Tony's custody, we don't want any of the money. We don't want the state to take him from us—"

"Jonas, wait just a minute." Tom leaned toward them, resting his elbows on the desktop. "The settlement with the insurance company has absolutely nothing to do with the judge's request for a progress report."

Robin felt her eyes blink stupidly.

"I thought I'd kept the issues separate in my letter," Tom went on. "I purposefully made the paragraph about the progress report short so it wouldn't worry you. You see, the court just wants to know how things are going. Anyone who is granted custody of a child must fill one out. It will take us all of ten minutes."

"I feel like an idiot," Jonas said softly. "I read about the money and the report, and I panicked."

"So did I," Robin said, wanting to take her share of the blame.

Jonas heaved a sigh. "You may have wanted to save us some worry by keeping the paragraph short, Tom—" he chuckled "—but we filled in the imaginary missing pieces by reading between the lines."

The lawyer shrugged. "There was nothing there to read."

"I guess we see that now," Jonas commented.

Questions plagued Robin ever since Jonas's letter had been mentioned. They swirled around in her brain until she was dizzy. She needed some answers. Now.

She turned to Jonas. "Can we talk?" Her question was quiet and utterly polite.

Tom jumped up from his chair. "I think that's a good idea," he said. "I'll go out and make a few phone calls." As he spoke he rounded his desk and made his way to the door of his office.

Before the door latch had even clicked closed, Robin said, "Why'd you do it, Jonas? Why'd you write that letter? Why didn't you tell me what you were doing? I thought we'd promised to be honest and up-front with each other."

"That was your promise," he said pointedly. "I told you I'd make everything okay. And I did what I could to do just that."

"But you were going to give up custody of Tony."

"So were you." There was a hint of accusation in his tone. "So much for being honest and up-front."

"I would have told you what I was going to do, but I didn't know I was going to do it until it was done."

He reached over and covered her hand with his. "I have to admit, I was worried there for a minute."

"Oh?"

Jonas nodded. "When you first spoke up about wanting a divorce, I thought you were lobbing the first bomb in our custody war."

"You had nothing to worry about," she assured him.

"I know that now. What I'm dying to know is why." He grasped her fingers tighter. "I know you want to raise him as much as I do. Why'd you offer to give me custody?"

Because I love you, she wanted to scream. But she couldn't open herself up to that degree. She glanced at the floor. "You two love each other. You deserve to be together. Tony needs you."

"You did it for Tony, then," he murmured.

She lifted her gaze and saw what she thought was disappointment in his green eyes, and she felt a moment of bewilderment.

"I'd hoped there was another reason."

There was a quality in his voice that made her pulse quicken. "You did?"

"Yes," he said. "But if there wasn't, then I need to just keep my proposition to myself."

"Proposition? What proposition?" She felt like a mimicking parrot who couldn't come up with words on her own.

He slid to one side of the seat until his knees pressed against hers.

"Seeing as how we're both willing to give up our rights to Tony," he said, "when we both want those rights very much, don't you think that means something? Don't you think there must be some other reason we're willing to give up what's most important to us?''

"Some other reason?" The question sounded breathy and lame to her. Her heart was pounding now.

"Besides doing it for Tony's sake, I mean?"

Her tongue darted out to moisten her dry lips, and she searched his face. She waited for him to continue, and when he didn't, she realized that he was waiting for some response from her, some sign to tell him she was open to following him along the path he was heading down.

"Maybe," she said. "Maybe there is some other reason."

There was tightly suppressed jubilance in his eyes now. An infectious happiness that had her lips curling into a gentle smile.

His whole demeanor changed. She could see the tenseness easing from his shoulders. She watched as the worry seemed to melt from his face. He was once again the confident man she'd fallen in love with.

"So," she said, "tell me about this proposition of yours."

"Okay. I propose that we raise Tony together," he said. "But there's a catch."

Her raised brows displayed her curiosity.

"Mmm-hmm," he said. "I say we raise Tony together, live in the same house, but as true man and wife this time."

She wanted to slide into his lap and hug him to her. She wanted to shout, "Yes!" to his proposition. But she decided not to just yet. Not until she'd gotten the chance to do something she'd been dying to do.

"I don't know," she said, keeping her tone as serious as possible.

His smile faded, and Robin nearly laughed.

"How do I know what kind of husband you'll make?" she asked. "I mean, we've only lived together as coguardians of Tony. How do I know if we can make it as...husband and wife?"

The look on his face was worth a thousand words. It was all she could do to keep from chuckling. She'd really put one over on him. And she'd wanted to do it ever since he'd left her splayed across that mountain of lemons in the grocery store. Dear Lord, but this felt good!

"But then," she went on, reaching up to tap her chin with her index finger, "I *do* know that you're awfully good in bed."

His green eyes widened, and at the same time, her face flamed red-hot. She couldn't believe she'd actually had the nerve to say that! But seeing his surprise was hysterical.

"You're teasing me." His tone was filled to the brim with incredulity.

She finally gave in to her urge to laugh.

"I can't believe it," he said. "You've found a sense of humor."

Robin knew her eyes were glistening merrily.

Jonas seemed to realize suddenly the topic on which she'd chosen to jest. His smile disappeared completely.

"I'm not certain I like being the butt of your jokes," he told her.

"Is that so?" she asked. She shifted her position until she was planted firmly in his lap. The feel of his hands as they slid around her waist was wonderful.

"You may as well get used to it," she said. "Because I've spent weeks taking lessons from the best."

"The best, huh?" he murmured, tipping up his chin so he could nibble on her earlobe.

"The best," she repeated softly.

She turned her head and kissed his mouth. His lips tasted sweet, delectable, and she was overcome with the feeling of starvation. It felt as if she'd wanted this forever. Wanted to taste his kiss, feel his hands on her body.

"I love you," he whispered softly against her lips.

Those three little words were the most beautiful ones she had ever heard. "I love you," she said.

They got lost in the heated energy that pulsed around them. His fingertips grazed her breast and she parted her lips, inviting him to deepen the kiss.

There was a quick knock at the door and Tom poked his head into the room.

"Oh," he said, "I guess you two have worked things out."

When he didn't get an answer, he straightened up, turned to his secretary and murmured, "Maybe we should take an early lunch."

Once the door had closed softly, Jonas pulled back and gazed into Robin's face.

"Tell me something," he said. "When you joked earlier about my prowess in the bedroom, was it a joke you meant, or a joke you didn't mean?"

She thought it was so sexy to see that tiny hint of uncertainty in a man she knew to be extremely self-confident.

"Tell you what—" she kissed him softly on the cheek "—I'll let you know as soon as we get home."

Epilogue

"Why did I let you talk me into this?"

Robin pushed herself from the front seat of the car and stood on the curb until Jonas had unbuckled Tony from his car seat.

She placed her hand on her very pregnant belly. "I'm fat," she pronounced miserably.

Jonas kissed her mouth. He put a protective hand on top of the one she had on her stomach. "You're beautiful," he said.

He carried two-year-old Tony in one arm and held Robin's hand in his, and all together they started off toward the little church up the street.

Suddenly she lamented, "I'm waddling down Main Street like a duck."

Tony's eyes lit up. "I could have a duck!"

"No," Jonas said patiently, "you can't have a duck. In about two weeks we're going to have a *baby*."

The child's bottom lip pooched out. "I want a duck."

"I don't understand why he doesn't understand," Jonas whispered to Robin.

"Our first mistake was in trying to explain it to him at all," she said.

Tony had spent the past three months shouting out randomly the things he'd much rather have other than a baby. She wasn't worried, though; she knew Tony would understand everything once the new baby arrived. Until then, she and Jonas would have to continue to explain what they could in the best way they knew how.

Her nephew had grown like a weed over the past ten months. And she still marveled at how quickly he learned.

Even though she felt uncomfortable now that she was in the final stages of her pregnancy, she knew she had never been happier in her life.

She reached up and fingered a longish lock of Jonas's silky hair. He needed to have it cut again. If it wasn't for her reminding him every few months, she was sure he'd probably let it grow until he tripped on it. She smiled gently. That was okay with her, she loved him just the way he was.

The gentle wind tugged at the veil she had pinned to her hair and she absently raised her hand to steady it.

"A white veil," she muttered. She looked down at her pretty, flowered maternity dress. Jonas had wanted her to wear a white gown when they repeated their vows in front of Reverend Walsh, but she'd stood firm and had only relented by wearing the snowy and billowing headpiece he'd picked out. She chuckled at the memory of how he'd argued with her.

"There's nothing virginal about a pregnant bride," she said to him now.

"Remember," he told her, a twinkle of humor in his eye, "the state already considers you an honest woman. Our quickie wedding was completely legal. We're only going to repeat our vows to the minister."

"Yeah, but half these people out here on the street don't know that," she muttered. "They're looking at me like I'm crazy."

"I know," he said. "Isn't it great?"

She refrained from growling at him.

"And I'm glad I talked you into this before you had the baby."

There was a question in Robin's gaze as she waited for him to explain.

"I wouldn't want to become a daddy before I had the chance to walk down the aisle."

This time she did growl at him.

The roar of a jet engine high overhead drew their nephew's rapt attention.

"How 'bout a plane?" Tony suddenly blurted. "I could have a plane."

She and Jonas laughed together. He held open the heavy wooden door of the church and she waddled inside with her loving family close behind her.

*   *   *   *   *

The first book in the exciting new
Fortune's Children series is

HIRED HUSBAND

by *New York Times* bestselling writer
Rebecca Brandewyne

Beginning in July 1996
Only from Silhouette Books

Here's an exciting sneak preview....

Minneapolis, Minnesota

As Caroline Fortune wheeled her dark blue Volvo into
the underground parking lot of the towering, glass-and-
steel structure that housed the global headquarters of
Fortune Cosmetics, she glanced anxiously at her gold Pi-
aget wristwatch. An accident on the snowy freeway had
caused rush-hour traffic to be a nightmare this morning.
As a result, she was running late for her 9:00 a.m. meeting—and if there was one thing her grandmother, Kate
Winfield Fortune, simply couldn't abide, it was slack, un-
professional behavior on the job. And lateness was the sign
of a sloppy, disorganized schedule.

Involuntarily, Caroline shuddered at the thought of her
grandmother's infamous wrath being unleashed upon her.
The stern rebuke would be precise, apropos, scathing and
delivered with coolly raised, condemnatory eyebrows and
a icy tones of haughty grandeur that had in the past re-
duced many an executive—even the male ones—at Fortune Cosmetics not only to obsequious apologies, but even
to tears. Caroline had seen it happen on more than one
occasion, although, much to her gratitude and relief, she
herself was seldom a target of her grandmother's anger.
And she wouldn't be this morning, either, not if she could
help it. That would be a disastrous way to start out the new
year.

Grabbing her Louis Vuitton totebag and her black
leather portfolio from the front passenger seat, Caroline

stepped gracefully from the Volvo and slammed the door
The heels of her Maud Frizon pumps clicked briskly on th
concrete floor as she hurried toward the bank of elevator
that would take her up into the skyscraper owned by he
family. As the elevator doors slid open, she rushed dow
the long, plushly carpeted corridors of one of the hushe
upper floors toward the conference room.

By now Caroline had her portfolio open and was lea
ing through it as she hastened along, reviewing her note
she had prepared for her presentation. So she didn't see D
Nicolai Valkov until she literally ran right into him. Lik
her, he had his head bent over his own portfolio, no
watching where he was going. As the two of them co
lided, both their portfolios and the papers inside went fly
ing. At the unexpected impact, Caroline lost her balanc
stumbled, and would have fallen had not Nick's strong
sure hands abruptly shot out, grabbing hold of her an
pulling her to him to steady her. She gasped, startled an
stricken, as she came up hard against his broad chest, lea
hips and corded thighs, her face just inches from his own—
as though they were lovers about to kiss.

Caroline had never been so close to Nick Valkov be
fore, and, in that instant, she was acutely aware of him—
not just as a fellow employee of Fortune Cosmetics b
also as a man. Of how tall and ruggedly handsome he wa
dressed in an elegant, pin-striped black suit cut in th
European fashion, a crisp white shirt, a foulard tie and
pair of Cole Haan loafers. Of how dark his thick, gloss
hair and his deep-set eyes framed by raven-wing brow
were—so dark that they were almost black, despite th
bright, fluorescent lights that blazed overhead. Of th
whiteness of his straight teeth against his bronzed skin a
a brazen, mocking grin slowly curved his wide, sensua
mouth.

"Actually, I *was* hoping for a sweet roll this morning—
but I daresay you would prove even tastier, Ms. Fo

tune," Nick drawled impertinently, his low, silky voice tinged with a faint accent born of the fact that Russian, not English, was his native language.

At his words, Caroline flushed painfully, embarrassed and annoyed. If there was one person she always attempted to avoid at Fortune Cosmetics, it was Nick Valkov. Following the breakup of the Soviet Union, he had emigrated to the United States, where her grandmother had hired him to direct the company's research and development department. Since that time, Nick had constantly demonstrated marked, traditional, Old World tendencies that had led Caroline to believe he not only had no use for equal rights but also would actually have been more than happy to turn back the clock several centuries where females were concerned. She thought his remark was typical of his attitude toward women: insolent, arrogant and domineering. Really, the man was simply insufferable!

Caroline couldn't imagine what had ever prompted her grandmother to hire him—and at a highly generous salary, too—except that Nick Valkov was considered one of the foremost chemists anywhere on the planet. Deep down inside Caroline knew that no matter how he behaved, Fortune Cosmetics was extremely lucky to have him. Still, that didn't give him the right to manhandle and insult her!

"I assure you that you would find me more bitter than a cup of the strongest black coffee, Dr. Valkov," she insisted, attempting without success to free her trembling body from his steely grip, while he continued to hold her so near that she could feel his heart beating steadily in his chest—and knew he must be equally able to feel the erratic hammering of her own.

"Oh, I'm willing to wager there's more sugar and cream to you than you let on, Ms. Fortune." To her utter mortification and outrage, she felt one of Nick's hands slide insidiously up her back and nape to her luxuriant mass of sable hair, done up in a stylish French twist.

"You know so much about fashion," he murmured, eyeing her assessingly, pointedly ignoring her indignation and efforts to escape from him. "So why do you always wear your hair like this...so tightly wrapped and severe? I've never seen it down. Still, that's the way it needs to be worn, you know...soft, loose, tangled about your face. As it is, your hair fairly cries out for a man to take the pins from it, so he can see how long it is. Does it fall past your shoulders?" He quirked one eyebrow inquisitively, a mocking half smile still twisting his lips, letting her know he was enjoying her obvious discomfiture. "You aren't going to tell me, are you? What a pity. Because my guess is that it does—and I'd like to know if I'm right. And these glasses." He indicated the large, square, tortoiseshell frames perched on her slender, classic nose. "I think you use them to hide behind more than you do to see. I'll bet you don't actually even need them at all."

Caroline felt the blush that had yet to leave her cheeks deepen, its heat seeming to spread throughout her entire quivering body. Damn the man! Why must he be so infuriatingly perceptive?

Because everything that Nick suspected was true.

* * * * *

To read more, don't miss
HIRED HUSBAND
by Rebecca Brandewyne,
Book One in the new
FORTUNE'S CHILDREN series,
beginning this month and available only from
Silhouette Books!

New York Times Bestselling Author
REBECCA
BRANDEWYNE

Launches a new twelve-book series—FORTUNE'S CHILDREN
beginning in July 1996 with Book One

Hired Husband

Caroline Fortune knew her marriage to Nick Valkov was in
name only. She would help save the family business, Nick
would get a green card, and a paper marriage would suit both
of them. Until Caroline could no longer deny the feelings Nick
stirred in her and the practical union turned passionate.

MEET THE FORTUNES—a family whose legacy is greater than
riches. Because where there's a will...there's a wedding!

Look for Book Two, *The Millionaire and the Cowgirl*,
by Lisa Jackson. Available in August 1996 wherever Silhouette
books are sold.

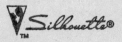

MILLION DOLLAR SWEEPSTAKES

This exciting new cross-line continuity series unites
five of your favorite authors as they weave five
connected novels about love, marriage—and
Daddy's unexpected need for a baby carriage!

Get ready for

THE BABY NOTION by Dixie Browning (SD#1011, 7/96)
Single gal Priscilla Barrington would do anything for a
baby—even visit the local sperm bank. Until cowboy
Jake Spencer set out to convince her to have a family
the natural—and much more exciting—way!

And the romance in New Hope, Texas, continues with:

BABY IN A BASKET
by Helen R. Myers (SR#1169, 8/96)

MARRIED...WITH TWINS!
by Jennifer Mikels (SSE#1054, 9/96)

HOW TO HOOK A HUSBAND (AND A BABY)
by Carolyn Zane (YT#29, 10/96)

DISCOVERED: DADDY
by Marilyn Pappano (IM#746, 11/96)

DADDY KNOWS LAST arrives in July...only from

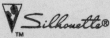

Who can resist a Texan...or a Calloway?

This September, award-winning author
ANNETTE BROADRICK
returns to Texas, with a brand-new
story about the Calloways...

CLINT: The brave leader. Used to keeping secrets.

CADE: The Lone Star Stud. Used to having women
fall at his feet...

MATT: The family guardian. Used to handling
trouble...

They must discover the identity of the mystery
woman with Calloway eyes—and uncover a
conspiracy that threatens their family....

Look for **SONS OF TEXAS: Rogues and Ranchers**
in September 1996!

Only from Silhouette...where passion lives.

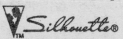

You're About to Become a *Privileged Woman*

Reap the rewards of fabulous free gifts and benefits with proofs-of-purchase from Silhouette and Harlequin books

Pages & Privileges™

It's our way of thanking you for buying our books at your favorite retail stores.

PROOF OF PURCHASE
SR-PP155
Offer expires October 31, 1996

Harlequin and Silhouette— the most privileged readers in the world!

For more information about Harlequin and Silhouette's PAGES & PRIVILEGES program call the Pages & Privileges Benefits Desk: 1-503-794-2499

Silhouette®

SR-PP155